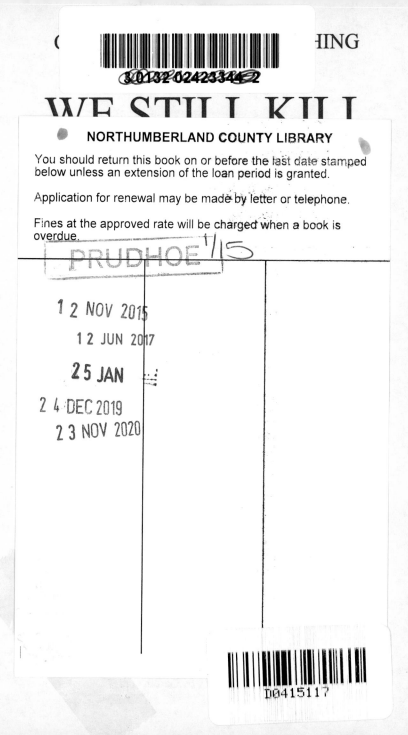

C⋯⋯HING

‖‖‖‖‖‖‖‖‖‖‖‖‖‖‖‖‖

30132 02423344 2

WE STILL KILL

‖‖‖‖‖‖‖‖‖‖‖‖‖‖‖‖‖

D0415117

Published by Caffeine Nights Publishing 2014

Published in Great Britain by Caffeine Nights Publishing

www.caffeine-nights.com

British Library Cataloguing in Publication Data.

A CIP catalogue record for this book is available from the British Library

ISBN: 978-1-907565-84-7

Cover design by

David Laird

Artworked by
Mark (Wills) Williams

Everything else by
Default, Luck and Accident

Photography by Gareth Gatrell

'This one's for Jonathan Sothcott at Richwater Films and Darren Laws at Caffeine Nights, who both narrowed their eyes and said, 'Yeah, okay, let's give it a shot.'

Thanks guys.'

Foreword Ian Ogilvy & Jonathan Sothcott

So there I was sitting at home in California - yes, poor old me - moaning to my wife about the chronic shortage of good old men's roles - and come to that the chronic shortage of lousy old men's roles too - when out of the blue my agent sends me a script and asks if I'd be at all interested in the part of Richie Archer in this British gangster film? And I thought 'This is probably a little cough-and-a-spit of a role - a one day or a two day job at best - I probably die on the third page' - then I read the script and discovered that Richie Archer doesn't die, he's the dramatic centre of the film, it's the leading part, that it's wonderfully written, that it's the sort of thing I've never done before and that I don't have to audition for it - it's an actual offer for God's sake! - and I jump up whooping with delight and my wife says 'I see you've stopped moaning, then?' and I say Bloody right old girl.'

I was on the next plane out of Los Angeles.

Ian Ogilvy
Los Angeles 2014

MAKING A FILM... THE OLD WAY

Around the beginning of the year I was, as one should be at the beginning of all showbusiness anecdotes, sat in a pub in Soho, talking about two films with two chaps after a few beers. However, these particular chaps were high flying film distributors, the type red tops refer to as 'movie bosses' and they had come to ask me to make a movie for them. They had a title – We Still Kill The Old Way – and a concept, which was Krays era London gangsters coming out of retirement to clean up the streets. Having just made Vendetta, a sort of Death Wish in London, which had been very successful, but being focred to wait until its star (Danny Dyer) got a break in his Eastenders schedule to make Vendetta 2, making another revenge movie seemed like a great idea. I had some reservations – how do you make this kind of un-PC gangster likeable but once director Sacha Bennett came on board such doubts soon vanished and we started the most fun part of any movie – casting.

Casting We Still Kill The Old Way was basically opening the toy box of my film and TV childhood and getting out all the best toys. The first actor on board was Chris Ellison – Frank Burnside in The Bill, surely in the running as TV's greatest cop. Next up was 80s screen siren Lysette Anthony, just as sizzling today as when I first saw her opposite Michael Caine in Without A Clue in 1987. Sacha and I flew to Dublin to meet Indiana Jones goddess Alison Doody (my favourite Bond girl) who was an unexpected coup. Impossibly glamorous and sophisticated, Ali is famously picky about which jobs she takes so her coming on board felt like a real endorsement of the material. Steven Berkoff, an old mate came and did us a favour. Danny Dyer called me from Eastenders – I should look at a young lad called Danny-Boy

Hatchard who'd just been cast as his son. He was perfect for our villain and delivers a real breakout performance. We changed one of his footsoldiers from a boy to a girl just because I wanted to work with Kidulthood actress Red Madrell – again she was amazing. And then I called Dyer and sounded him out about his daughter Dani playing the young female lead: she'd done a day on Vendetta and blown us all away. It was a gamble because all the crew knew he and I are close, but I'd never have taken it unless I knew she could pull it off and boy did she deliver.

So all this was endless joy but throughout the process Sacha and I faced one incredible obstacle. We couldn't find a leading man. Every idea we came up with seemed to end in "he's dead" – Lewis Collins, Edward Woodward, our ideas were all three years out of date. Then Martin Kemp called me one night watching some old series on TV "what about Ian Ogilvy?" he asked. Eureka! Because he'd been based out of LA for twenty years he hadn't been on our radar. Of course there was no budget for flights but Sacha and I halved our white wine bill for a week and a deal was done... The Saint was on a plane (hmmm Saints On A Plane, there's a film idea there somewhere).

And Ogilvy was just majestic – we could never have hoped for better. Commanding, tough, debonair and incredibly charismatic, he gives the performance of his career. I went to Spain with him and his mate Nicky Henson for location filming and had the most wonderful three days, he's just utterly brilliant. I really didn't want him to go home.

They say that the jobs you have the most fun on are the ones the public enjoy the least but early word on WSKTOW is very positive and I have to say I'm incredibly proud of it. Of course, making a good film isn't enough. The press usually give my films a mauling but then I don't make them for the press. I think this one's a bit different though – it's certainly the classiest film I've ever made: I think the like of Ogilvy, Doody, Anthony, James Cosmo et al give it a veneer of respectability that your average geezer film lacks and it has a certain dark humour that I think audiences will find satisfying. The cast add a real grit and realism too which balances it out nicely. I'm not a betting man by nature but I'd put a bullseye on a sequel being greenlit and we already have a concept. We'll find out when it's released in December.

One of the joys of making these films is the novelisations released by Caffeine Nights. My friend Nick Oldham did such a great job of adapting the Vendetta screenplay that he was the only choice to novelise We Still Kill The Old Way. You now hold the result in your hands – he's done a fantastic job and I hope you'll enjoy reading it as much as I did.

Jonathan Sothcott
London 2014

LONDON: Postcode E2
Latitude 51.52 degrees
Longitude - 0.06 degrees

ONE

They were on the prowl, even though it was still daylight.

Their hunting ground was a tower block, a seventies throwback, the last one left standing from a cluster of four, the other three having been demolished, their remains yet to be bulldozed away. It stood alone amongst huge mounds of hardcore, a target. Tall, ugly and unforgiving, designed by over-paid planners and architects who believed that high-rise was the answer to society's woes; that the inhabitants would enjoy living right next to and on top of each other. That communities would prosper and come together and be strong.

Not, as happened, fracture. And the people would become isolated and afraid, and once well-lit stairwells and concrete walkways and working lifts, all designed to aid community spirit and put people in touch with people, would become places of fear where criminality and drug abuse became rife, gang culture thrived. And the concrete itself, the bedrock which bonded these communities would, in an ironic metaphor, begin to rot away, cracks would show into which cockroaches could scuttle to hide away and the fabric of the tower blocks would disintegrate, just like their inhabitants.

And the E2 were on the hunt. Hoodies tugged over their heads, the features of their faces dark and blurred except for the occasional time when the light caught their eyes and they looked like zombies from hell.

This place, the last of the tower blocks in this area was easy pickings for them because it was as if the remaining occupants of the flats had been abandoned to their fate by uncaring authorities until the explosives had done their work, the bulldozers had moved in and the people re-housed.

Today there were nine members of the gang.

On another day it could have been sixteen, on another, five. The numbers varied, but there were never less than four.

Numbers gave them strength, courage and the audacity to take on anyone. That was how the E2 worked – as a team with a leader.

They had started on the ground floor, then worked their way up the stairwells, silently moving around each walkway, hoping to stumble across an easy victim on the way to their target. But the residents were all locked in behind secure doors and the only takings were from a stoned-out druggie on the third floor who they rolled for a tenner in his pocket and a tiny sachet of coke. Their instinct was then to hurl him down the steps, but the gang leader stepped in and stopped them. Not because he would not have enjoyed the spectacle, but because they were here for something else.

Eventually they reached the tenth floor.

It was on this level they would find their target, a flat they knew would be unoccupied for a couple of hours at least. The leader knew this because he had been fed the information by their sub-gang of watchers. These were the kids considered too young to run with the main gang (although the ages of that gang ran anywhere from ten to twenty-five); the sub-gang were the kids who wanted to earn their creds. They did this by feeding information to the gang leader by text messages and photographs by phone.

This was how he knew about flat number 1020. Tenth floor, flat twenty.

At the top of the stairs the gang leader held up his hand. The eight others stopped behind him, a line of them snaking down the concrete stairs, silently looking up at him. He glanced around at them, a self-satisfied sneer on his face.

His gang. His minions. His orders.

His violence.

His name was Aaron.

He checked his smartphone, looked at the photo he'd been sent twenty minutes earlier of the front door of the flat. The gang were on the right level and by turning left on the walkway, 1020 was fourth along according to directions, which were rarely wrong. Aaron knew that the sub-gang were dotted across the estate, ready to warn him if the old guy who lived at the flat came home unexpectedly. Because that was the thing – it was easy and safer to break into empty flats because if the occupiers were at home, most of the front doors were now barred with heavy locks and bolts which, of course, could not be set if the owner was out.

Aaron glanced down the line.

He looked at Maz, one of the youths behind him. 'You got it?'

'Yuh.' Maz held up the steel bodied, iron-headed door-ram, the type used by cops to smash open doors when raiding houses. In fact, it was exactly the same as a police ram because Maz had lifted it out of the back of an unoccupied police personnel carrier about a month earlier. Stupid bastards had left the vehicle unlocked whilst they were all tied up with a mini-riot on an adjoining estate. Maz had stolen it and at the same time done a very sloppy shit and then urinated on the driver's seat before escaping. It had been one of those pure joy moments which he had also captured on camera.

Today was the first time of its use.

Aaron jerked his head and Maz ran up the stairs to the head of the gang, drawing one or two envious glares from some of the others, all of which Maz noticed and acknowledged superciliously. He was one of Aaron's right hand men, a lieutenant, an enviable position to hold.

'You practised with that fucker?' Aaron asked about the door-ram.

'Smashed in me Granddad's shed door.'

'Silly cunt,' Aaron laughed. He put his phone away, his head twisted to the others. 'You lot ready? Then let's get fuckin' moving.'

Even though he was pumped up and feeling ferocious, Aaron – with Maz just ahead of him – led the gang quietly along the walkway to the flat door, standing with his back to the wall. Leroy, another of Aaron's lieutenants, took up a position on the opposite side of the door.

Maz lined up the door-ram, swung it back and forth a few times to create some momentum – because the tool was a lot heavier than it looked – and also to get his eye in, his balance right, and hit the door at the place where it would be most effective.

A murmur went through the gang: excitement.

Maz swung it again and this time smashed the door by the main lock. The door rattled, but did not open.

'Shit.'

Maz glanced sheepishly at Aaron who voiced what the rest of the gang were thinking. 'Wanker.'

Maz's face hardened with determination. He repositioned himself, swung back the ram and pounded it accurately against the door which split with a crack. Maz followed this up by flat-footing it, sending it splintering, crashing back on its hinges, revealing the hallway of flat 1020 beyond.

They were in.

***

This was one of Richie Archer's most favourite times of day. It wasn't cool, but the fierce heat had gone out of the Spanish sun and it was possible to wander around without having to worry too much about the effects of the sun's rays. It was now that he liked to spend some time pottering around his garden, trimming the trees and bushes, keeping on top of their growth.

He had been fighting with a particularly nasty palm bush, the sharp jagged teeth of its tough leaves that protected the dates having cut into his hands and forearms as he hacked them back, then threw the scimitar-like leaves into the compost pile in the far corner of the garden.

Richie rose up, stretching his aching back, literally licking his wounds whilst taking in the magnificent vista from his villa. The slowly sinking, huge orange ball of the sun dropping below the horizon, the shadows lengthening across the silver and azure blue of the Mediterranean, silhouettes of boats large dotted along the horizon.

He paused to consider the nature of it all, astounded by it every day.

He sucked blood from his thumb, then spat it out, grinned wryly and said to himself, 'Me, pottering about in a fucking garden ... the lads'd kill 'emselves chuntering at that ... if only they knew.'

That thought made his face harden. And he had a handsome face, craggy and deeply suntanned now. That and his well-toned body belied the fact he was approaching seventy years of age. He looked much younger and still had the air of a grey wolf in its prime about him.

He turned away from the view, suddenly feeling the urge to do something a little outrageous, maybe dangerous, definitely fun.

He walked past the infinity swimming pool to the small brick building in the far corner of the garden that housed the pool pump and water pump that supplied the villa. He unlocked it and ducked under the door, then immediately turned on his heels in the confined space and reached above the door. In a specially constructed space chipped into the stone roof supporting joist, he lifted the hinged lid of this hiding place, feeling with his fingers until they closed over what he sought.

He smiled grimly as he lifted out a sawn-off shotgun.

***

They exploded through the door as though fired from a rocket, into the staid hallway, led by Aaron swaggering like some kind of invincible fighting force. Leroy and Maz were at his shoulders, with DK following up, then the rest of the gang who split aggressively into the rooms off the hall, a bedroom, bathroom, spare room.

Aaron stepped into the living room, then paused to survey it with a disappointed look on his face.

'Little pig, little pig, let me come in,' he said. They were like words from a children's nursery rhyme, but his tone twisted them malevolently as they came out of his mouth.

The room was not large, even though this flat with its two bedrooms was one of the larger ones in the block. It had a very dated feel to it, old fashioned patterned carpets, worn and threadbare. The settee and armchair did not match, but had once been plush and comfortable. Now they were worn and flat with springs jutting out. There was a huge, ancient TV on a table, deep and wide with a tube and an old VCR player stacked underneath it, a pile of video cassettes next to it – old crime and cowboy films.

This was clearly the home of an old person.

Aaron's voice trailed off as he surveyed the room, then he nodded at DK, the only female member of the gang – but just as hard and uncompromising as any of the lads, and simmering with a violent sexuality which terrified most males.

On Aaron's nod, she screamed, 'E2 – let's do our thing.'

On this command the gang set upon and began to destroy the fixtures and fittings of the house, side-swiping ornaments from shelves, hunting through cupboards, smashing anything they did not like the look of, but collecting and piling up anything that could be valuable in the middle of the living room carpet.

Maz smashed the TV screen with the door ram. It exploded spectacularly.

Leroy took out a tin of spray paint and started to spray obscenities on the wall and paintings whilst JP, one of the youngest gang members leapt onto the double bed and pissed all over it, especially the pillows.

Aaron swaggered cockily through the ongoing carnage, egging on his gang, urging them to do as much damage as possible. This was good. This was the goal. Destruction. It felt good and gave him a throbbing erection and a huge feeling of power. He controlled it all. He was the man.

He stood before a series of framed photographs lined up on top of an old, glass fronted cabinet containing a variety of pottery ornaments. He bent and looked into the faces of the people in the pictures, rubbing a hand over his crotch as he stood there.

Maz stepped forwards in front of Dean – the one gang member who seemed uncomfortable by the wanton destruction – picked up one and drove a particularly nasty looking knife into the faces of the children in that photo – someone's grand kids. Then he swept the others off the cabinet and danced on them, smashing them to pieces.

He turned to Aaron, who nodded approvingly.

***

The villa stood in its own grounds, nestling in an area of two acres lovingly tended by Richie himself and a gardener who came three times a week to mow the lawns. Richie loved the process of maintaining it, found a lot of peace and tranquillity in so doing ... calming the nerves and urges of the savage beast which lurked within him and which, sometimes, needed to be unleashed.

Like today.

With the shotgun he had climbed over the rear garden wall and walked to a position about a hundred yards away from the villa (because Richie still firmly calculated everything in Imperial measure, not metric despite residing in Spain). Here he'd glanced back at the villa, a pride in what he saw, but also aware of the metaphor the villa seemed to represent and say about him. It stood resolute, somewhat isolated, surrounded on three sides by a virtual wasteland of about twenty acres that Richie also owned.

He had bought the land at the same time as the villa, both at a knock-down price, over twenty years before.

Even then, Richie had seen the benefit of the villa's location, nearest town about five miles distant, away from prying eyes, somewhere he could live a peaceful existence but which would also be in a position to defend if necessary.

The problem at the time of purchase was that the villa was the first to be built on what was destined to become an exclusive estate.

Richie had wanted the villa but not the prospective neighbours, which was why had had bought the surrounding land, much to the chagrin of the property developer who did not want to sell it.

Richie smiled grimly at that memory.

Negotiations with the developer had been tense, to say the least. But in the end Richie had made the Spaniard see sense and even sell the land at a very cheap price indeed. Richie could still see the beads of sweat rolling down the man's anguished face as his bloodied fingers held the pen that signed the deeds over to Richie. This was all witnessed, of course, by a fully legal Spanish solicitor. Richie's solicitor.

This gave Richie the land, the house and the isolation he craved at that time, and it was where he had lived ever since.

Now and then, though, he needed that blast from the past, just to keep his eye in. Hence the shotgun, which was only one of several weapons secreted in and around the villa.

He had been watching and nurturing a particular cactus in the scrubland. It was one of those he remembered seeing in cowboy films when he was a lad, rather like a fat, green, prickly cop, holding up his hands in submission.

As much as he liked plants, Richie had always known that one day, this big cactus would meet its maker.

He opened the shotgun – a present from a certain Sicilian he had met in the late 60's over fifty gold bars – and threaded two cartridges into the side-by-side barrels, then snapped the weapon shut. He paused, then reopened it, then shut it, then opened, then shut it. Three times: the story of his life.

He was ready.

He held the shotgun at hip level and blasted the head off the cactus. The buckshot ripped through the tough outer layer, then ripped into its soft spongy flesh and tore the plant into a thousand tiny chunks, splattering it across the barren ground, leaving only a jagged, pulpy mess which could just as easily as anything have been a man's neck, the head having been severed.

Richie remained motionless, something inside him not quite satisfied by this little demonstration. His right eyelid twitched three times.

He fully broke open the shotgun and ejected the two spent cartridges onto the dry earth.

***

Aaron had been the one to find the safe, wall mounted at the back of a fitted wardrobe in the main bedroom. He had got a couple of the gang to jemmy it off its hidden brackets then carry it through to the lounge and deposit it in the middle of the floor.

To the same gang members he said, 'Open the fucker.'

They set about it with savage gusto.

It was nothing high-end, just a shop bought electronic digital safe with an LCD display, a keypad and an actual key that opened double locking steel bolts. The gang didn't even try to work through any digital combinations, but by using the jemmies and hammers, they beat the valiant contraption into submission until it finally lost its battle and the door swung open.

Fortunately it had the last laugh.

It was empty.

'Wank!' Aaron uttered, but then shook his head, made a decision: it was time to get out of this place. 'Get everything, then we go.'

They bagged all portable valuables as Aaron stepped back into the hall, a self-satisfied smirk on his face. There wasn't really much of value to steal but everything was worth something to a dealer and he was happy enough … until he glanced down the hall and saw the young woman gawping at him through the open front door. He stopped abruptly and his smile dropped.

She was just another resident awaiting relocation, hopefully to a better place. A single mother out with her kiddie in a pushchair, doing her best to put food into the child's mouth, keep out of harm's way and live in peace. But she also felt protective of the other residents in the block who had to tolerate this gang related shit daily, something they did not deserve, especially the nice old geezer at 1020.

For a moment, she was fierce. She moved her child in the pushchair to one side and demanded, 'What the fuck are you doing?' to Aaron.

His mouth snarled as he pushed his way past his gang, walking on the balls of his feet, and marched up to the young girl. Her name was Gemma.

She cowered, her mettle drying up under his hostile approach.

'What the fuck it got to do with you?'

She backed off, scared, but Aaron was never the sort to let a situation fizzle out if he had the upper hand. He was the type who believed in stamping his authority on every person who feared him. Gemma turned to retreat, pushing the pram quickly away. Aaron contorted out of the front door, reached past her and grabbed the pushchair handle.

'Please, I don't want…' she started to beg.

He was next to her now. 'Shut up, slut,' he said, peeling her fingers off the pushchair handle and as he did this he continued to growl in a low voice, 'It's lucky you're fucking ugly, otherwise I'd bend you over those railings and give you another fucking ugly bastard to feed.'

As he spoke, the E2 began to file past as they left the flat, cackling at her, blowing kisses.

Aaron now had hold of both her hands, squeezing them painfully, bending her fingers back.

'Did you see anything here?' he said.

'No … no … I don't know what you…'

'Tell you what, slut … let's make sure you're deaf, blind and dumb, eh?'

He flicked her hands out of his grasp, snatched up the pushchair with the baby fastened inside it, then hauled it over the balcony railings, ten floors to the ground below, letting it dangle there. The baby began to scream as Aaron shook the pushchair roughly.

Gemma, horrified, but now driven by the protective maternal urge inside her, attempted to grab the pram, but she hadn't seen Maz behind her. He forced her back against the outside wall of the flat, a knife suddenly in his right hand, his left arm slammed diagonally across her chest. He held the long blade of the knife across her throat. One hard 'zip' and her blood would have flowed.

Aaron peered over the railings, still dangling the pram perilously. He twisted to look at Gemma. 'Would you recognise me if you saw me again?'

Stunned by the terror and violence of the situation and the abject fear she felt for the life of her child, she could not form any coherent words.

Aaron said, 'Answer is, no you wouldn't, you couldn't.'

Thinking he would be satisfied by a nod, she dipped her head whilst dry-gasping through her tears.

'No, say it!' Aaron screamed.

'I … I didn't see you,' she squeaked. 'Or anyone. I don't know who you are … I don't…'

Aaron smiled with grim triumph. 'Now I believe you.'

He lugged the pushchair back over the railings to safety and threw it onto the walkway with no thought for the child. He strutted away whilst Maz slowly released Gemma, using the hand that had pinned her to the wall to grab one of her breasts and give it a hard tweak, his pleasure perverse. He sneered at her and giggled horribly before picking up the door-ram he'd put on the floor then scuttled after his leader, the person he admired most in the world. Once he caught up, he said, 'What now, bruv?'

Aaron strutted along, his shoulders rolling with his cocksure gait. He was full of himself, pumped up yet still dissatisfied.

'After all that, I need to teach a bitch how to suck this.' He stopped abruptly, Maz almost crashing into him. He grabbed his crotch to demonstrate what he meant. The bulge under Aaron's tracksuit bottoms was still clear to see. He was now pent up with sexual frustration.

Further back down the walkway, Gemma was kneeling in front of the pushchair, trying to calm her child who, fortunately, had no conception of how close to death he had been, but was still upset by the rough shaking and harsh voices. Gemma saw Aaron grasping his cock whilst looking at her, which sent a shockwave of intense hatred and fear through her.

But he wasn't thinking about Gemma, who meant nothing to him.

'Which one?' Maz asked, grinning dirtily.

'That Lauren skank.'

Maz had obviously expected a different answer and hearing the name Lauren puzzled him. 'Thought she wasn't putting it out, frigid bitch, int she?'

As if this was some kind of slur against his manhood, Aaron reacted angrily. He slammed Maz against the wall and from nowhere pulled out an extendable ASP baton, whipping it open with a 'crack' to its full length. He forced the tip of it up into Maz's neck. Eyeball to eyeball, Aaron said, 'If I want something, I get it.'

Maz was now the one rigid with terror.

Aaron held the baton there a moment longer, but just as suddenly as he had turned on Maz, he let him go with a laugh at Maz's expense, as though he hadn't meant anything by the threat of violence.

'Chill the fuck out Maz, you pussy.' Aaron placed the tip of the baton against the wall and pushed it to retract it. He slid the weapon away just as quickly as he had made it appear, then stepped back and adopted a stance as though he was revealing something marvellous. 'Look at me … girls will do anything to get a piece of this.'

Once more, he grabbed his crotch.

***

The headphones were even more sensitive than a doctor's stethoscope. Richie put them on carefully, removed them, put them back on, took them off and finally, for the third time, they went back on and stayed on.

He went slowly down onto his knees in front of the safe.

It was a square, heavy, free standing safe, quite modern in design with a plain black front on which was a combination dial. Richie's knees cracked as he lowered himself to his task.

He placed the listening aid for the headphones onto the safe door, paused, steadied himself, hardly breathing as he concentrated on listening to what the headphones were telling him.

He began to rotate the dial. Left, then right.

It took two minutes before he heard all four locking bolts withdraw with a subtle clunk and the safe door opened slightly. Richie leaned back and pulled the door fully open to reveal the inside of the completely empty safe.

He sighed, pleased by the skill and ease of entry, but also faintly dissatisfied by something he could not quite put his finger on.

He stood up, removed the headphones, placing them down on the coffee table, picking up a cup of tea and looking around at the circle of eight more safes of various models and degrees of difficulty that surrounded him.

TWO

'I never thought this would happen,' she said, deliriously happy.

'Well, babe, it's gonna,' Aaron said.

Lauren gasped as he pulled her roughly towards him and kissed her lips brutally, then backed her from the landing into the bedroom. He pressed himself against her and she could feel his rock hard cock against her belly.

As he rained kissed over her face and neck he pulled her tee shirt over her head and she raised her arms to facilitate this. He hurled the garment across the room, then expertly unfastened her bra, releasing her small breasts. Her hands went to his jeans, unbuttoning them quickly and working them down over his backside and revealing him. She took hold of him, causing a groan from somewhere deep in his throat and she liked that noise. It meant she was having the desired effect … and his penis felt immense and when she glanced down at it, she exhaled excitedly.

'Like what you see, like what you feel?' he wanted to know.

'Yeah.' She wriggled out of her tiny skirt, kicked it away.

He slid his hand down the front of her panties and inserted his middle finger into her, hard and painfully, no finesse.

'Nice pussy,' he said, and hissed the word, 'Tight.' He rotated her around, then sat on the edge of the bed, his cock curved hard up to his belly button. 'Suck me off,' he ordered her and jerked her down to her knees between his legs.

'But…' she started to protest, having expected something different. She had wanted it to be fast and exciting, a lot of clambering about, yes. In her dreams she had imagined herself straddling him, taking him inside her as they stared longingly into each other's eyes and climaxed together. Oral sex was something for the future, something to explore together as their love and intimacy grew to greater depths.

'Do it.' He cut her off and pushed her head down.

But that wasn't all. He didn't come in her mouth – for which she was somewhat grateful – but he hauled her onto the bed and went behind her, kneeling, adjusting her limbs, then parting the cheeks of her bottom as he thrust his member deep and hard into her and then came in a vicious, selfish, jerking orgasm that hurt her a lot, after which he rolled away and fell instantly asleep.

She lay awake, confused and not a little sore, then curled up, tears forming on the edge of her eyes as Aaron began snoring horribly.

***

Richie Archer stood in the hallway of his Spanish villa considering his reflection in the full length mirror by the front door. He rubbed his hands over his face, stretching his features, angling his head to look critically at himself, to get a measure of the man.

He wasn't far off seventy … it was certainly on the horizon, but the last twenty-odd years had been pretty good to him. Sure he'd aged. That was inevitable. Everyone did, no dodging that bullet. But he had looked after himself and it showed. Exercise, good diet and a healthy dose of controlled sunshine that had given him a deep tan which accentuated his rugged, handsome looks.

He allowed himself a smile, the corner of his mouth twitching.

'Not a bad old lag,' he congratulated himself, pleased enough by the reflection – until something caught his eye on the lapel of his otherwise impeccably clean and tailored linen jacket.

He frowned, annoyed. A piece of fluff. A tiny piece of fluff.

His manicured fingernails lifted it carefully off the material and he looked at it carefully before rolling it into a ball and placing it onto the hall table by the mirror.

Then he looked at himself again, adjusted the jacket which he buttoned, then unbuttoned … three times.

***

Detective Inspector Susan Taylor was a grafter, a driven force, and maybe someone who had forgotten how good looking she was because she spent her days with her genuine blonde hair scraped back off her face, wearing hardly any make up to speak of - and chasing killers.

At that moment in time she knew she was looking directly into the eyes of one, a killer, and a child killer at that. But at least she knew these were the last moments of an investigation that had lasted four months and reached its conclusion by the simple expedient of deploying a large number of very unwilling officers to do a fingertip search through a landfill site in Gravesend. Here she had found the damning receipt from the Subway sandwich shop in Bromley which put the killer and victim in the same place at the same time. From that point on the investigation had unravelled quicker than pulling a thread on one of her mother's home-knitted cardigans.

DC Graham Watts read out the charge of murder to the killer who, keeping his eyes locked dangerously with Taylor as she watched on, refused to respond. 'You are charged that on or about the 10th of April this year, you did murder Melissa Greene...'

With bail refused, Taylor took just one moment to step close to the prisoner and whisper, 'You will never see the outside of a prison again.'

'Fuck you, bitch,' he snarled, but was dragged away by a gaoler before he could spit into the DI's face, but he watched her over his shoulder until the very last moment.

She gave him a nice wave goodbye, then exhaled long and hard as exhaustion enveloped her.

DC Watts straightened the paperwork. 'Well done, boss.'

'And you. You worked hard on this, too.'

'You could've called it quits.'

She regarded the younger officer as if he had told a stupid joke. 'In the words of our greatest leader,' she said, 'Never, never, never, never give up.'

Watts frowned. 'Mrs Thatcher?'

Taylor shook her head sadly.

'You got time for a drink?' Watts asked hopefully. Taylor was two ranks higher than him, almost fifteen years older, but he had grand designs on her.

'What do you think, Graham?'

He gave a sad, thwarted smile.

***

Aaron had jerked awake, slurping back spittle that had dribbled out of the corner of his mouth. He was also in a bad mood, even when, having woken with an erection, he climbed onto Lauren and began to fuck her hard and dispassionately without even looking into her eyes. It took him a long time to climax and he did so with a ruthless thrusting that Lauren found painful and fairly unpleasant.

Then he was off the bed, naked, looking for something as Lauren sat up, watching him with a sheet pulled coyly up to her chin, covering her nakedness and looking every inch the pretty, innocent, nineteen year old girl she really was.

Aaron pulled on his clothing and drew his smartphone out of his jeans, then without even a glance in her direction, he headed to the door.

Lauren was stunned. 'Are you going already? Can't we … can't we cuddle or something? Talk?'

He stopped, turned slowly, almost as stunned as Lauren. 'Cuddle?' he said derisively. He shook his head. 'Nah, got more important things to do.'

'But…' She was lost for words for a moment. 'What about … us?' she asked delicately.

Aaron, sneering, sucked through his teeth. 'What are you chattin' about? There is no fucking "us."' He tweaked his fingers on the word 'us' to emphasise it. 'You're a sket, that's it, end of.'

'What d'you mean, sket? I am not,' she said defensively. Aaron just grinned and her face started to crumble. 'But all the time you spent with me, I thought…'

He shook his head. 'Tryin' to get you into bed, Lauren … waste of my time, going on the end result.'

She was completely dumbfounded by that and for a very brief moment her grip on the sheet loosened and she inadvertently exposed her left breast. Aaron snapped up his smartphone to capture the moment, but Lauren hastily pulled the sheet back up. Nevertheless he still took the photo.

'No! What are you doing?'

'Evidence, innit?'

A wave of something chilly and disturbing skittered through her. 'What do you mean?' she said suspiciously.

'Who'd believe I could get the ice queen into bed? My boys all think you're frigid.'

'Get out. GET OUT!' she cried.

Aaron stood by the bedroom door, chuckling and dialling a number on his phone which he put to his ear.

'Yo, Maz,' he said into the device, but with his eyes on Lauren. 'Mission accomplished.'

***

The telephone cable – which was in fact three cables connected together – stretched all the way out of the villa to the poolside. Richie sat on one of the chairs under the gazebo, phone to ear.

'Es el Senor Archer,' he was saying in reasonable, if halting, Spanish and with a big dollop of an East End accent to it. 'Una mesa pas dos esta noche.' He was on the line to his favourite restaurant. 'Si, si … me punto de visita habitual del mar … muchas gracias…' He was booking his usual table with sea views.

He placed the phone down, then picked it up to his ear … three times.

***

Susan Taylor would not have said that her latest case had affected her more deeply than any other. It had involved the death of a child and the hunt for the killer had been long and arduous and she had put in many hours. What she would have said was that she knew that sooner rather than later – probably

26

next day, this being the London she knew and loved so well –
she would be investigating another murder. She shuddered at
the prospect. Not because she disliked the job – quite the
opposite in fact, she loved it; she loved hunting down
murderers and looking into their eyes as the charge was read
out to them ... that was fucking brilliant.

Her problem was she needed a break.

She needed some time to chill, to reconnect, but also knew
that her annual leave was two months away and she was
beginning to wonder if she would make it that far because,
plain and simple, she was exhausted.

There was a very cold pint of Stella Artois in front of her.

She never drank out in a pub during the course of an
investigation, only when it was over and some evil bastard was
contemplating life on the wrong side of a cell door.

So tonight she was treating herself. But alone. She glanced
around the pub, a fairly typical boozer in this part of town. She
needed a bit of alone time. She looked at the beer, the bubbles
rising, the condensation rolling down the outside of the
bulbous Stella glass, and winced at the thought of DC Graham
Watts, who clearly fancied his chances at getting into her
knickers.

She actually smiled at the thought.

Watts was a nice lad, eager if slightly dim ... probably go
far, she thought wryly.

To be honest, the thought had crossed her mind, too. He was
pretty good looking and the prospect of his hard cock inside
her made her feel just a little bit ... moist.

But then another thought interrupted the slightly pleasing
prospect of having his balls cupped in her hand.

Her husband, Joe.

Someone, something, that always prevented her from doing
anything rash ... like sleeping with a junior officer.

'Shit,' she said, grabbed the beer and threw half of it down
her throat. It tasted wonderful as the icy fingers spread through
her chest.

***

Aaron was suitably impressed with Lauren's house. She had taken some persuading to bring him back here. Just into Bromley, it was really on the very periphery of his hunting ground. It was a modest, sixties semi and just … nice. He was impressed because as he searched the kitchen he had found a £10 note on one of the worktops, a nice ladies watch in a drawer, both of which he pocketed. As he searched cursorily around, his phone was clamped to his ear.

'Yeah, blud … she turned well dirty once I got her, y'know, lubricated.' He cackled filthily, looking for more items to steal easily. His eyes locked onto a framed photograph which he stepped close to and inspected closely, continuing to talk on the phone. 'Yeah, I'll see you at the place … gotta go.'

'What are you doing?'

Lauren stood at the kitchen door. Although Aaron had not noticed her, her appearance did not trouble him. He glanced at her and regarding the photograph asked, 'This your big sister?'

Lauren stepped into the kitchen, now fully clothed, her arms folded across her chest. 'It's my mum.'

'You need to introduce me to this peng mama…'

That was enough for Lauren. 'Can you just fucking leave?'

'You know what "peng" means, don't you? It's a fucking compliment, babe. I's complimentin' your mama … hot, sexy and be-yew-tiful.'

'Just leave,' Lauren said, stone faced, knowing exactly what peng meant.

'Hey – you be nice,' Aaron warned her, his smile evaporating. He made towards her. 'Or I'll be nasty.'

She shrank away from him, not knowing what to expect, but he caught her off guard and gently pulled her close to him, kissed her forehead tenderly, smiled with warmth and charm, totally confusing her.

'I'll call you, yeah?' He bent down to look in her eyes and she melted with a gasp. He touched her cheek gently with his fingertips, then was gone.

THREE

His motor was waiting for him outside Lauren's house, a result of one of the phone calls he had made. It was a ten year old BMW 3 series, badly painted matt black, basically the colour of a Teflon frying pan, the rear windows blacked out. The front windows were open and music throbbed out from the huge speakers fitted into the back parcel shelf. The body hung squat on wide, low-profile tyres, the flared wheel arches almost scraping the rubber off the tyres, but not quite.

Dean Walker, one of the E2 gang, had brought the car over at Aaron's behest and then slid over to the passenger seat to wait for the gang leader. As he waited, Dean rolled and lit a joint.

Aaron appeared down the side of Lauren's house, strutting down the garden path, dropping into the driver's seat and snatching the joint out of Dean's lips.

Dean accepted this without rancour. He knew the pecking order and he, Dean, was low in it. Dean looked at Aaron as he inhaled the pungent weed and held it in his lungs, then exhaled. He regarded him with respect and admiration because, at that moment in time, Dean idolised Aaron who he saw as a role model, someone to aspire to.

'Shit, Aaron,' Dean said suggestively, 'you took your time.'

Aaron had taken another lungful of smoke which he blew out pleasurably. 'I ain't like you,' he said with a smug grin, then gave Dean a sidelong squint, about to take the piss. 'See a girl and cum instantly.'

He roared with laughter as he flicked what remained of the joint out of the window as Dean coloured up. The accompanying roar of the badly tuned engine drowned out Dean's protest against his virility.

***

Richie Archer's car was much older than Aaron's BMW, almost forty years of age, but yet was much more stunning in its looks and still, despite the years, had high performance. It had cost Richie a lot of money to buy and cost an awful lot to maintain, but he never baulked at this because to him its style and what it represented was worth every penny.

He turned off the main coastal highway and followed the winding driveway up to the gravelled turning circle in front of the detached villa. He was very careful to loop around the gravel without kicking up any chippings onto the bodywork of the resplendent E-type Jaguar convertible, stopping close to the front steps of the villa and dipping his toe on the accelerator to rev the 5.3 litre V12 engine, which to Richie sounded like the roar of a mature male lion.

'Come on,' he shouted, smiling, and revved the engine again, watching the counter spin and, not for the first time, looking proudly at the golden plaque on the dashboard that identified this car as one of the last fifty to leave the production line.

He smiled wistfully at that. The end of what had been a British icon.

But at least he had a part of it.

The front door opened and the woman came out. She stood at the top of the steps, looking at Richie in a way that, he was certain, made his heart miss two beats at least.

To Richie she was the most beautiful woman in the world and he had lost his heart to her a long, long time ago.

Carmen was dark skinned with wide, brown eyes and jet black hair. She walked down the steps like a goddess and Richie felt himself welling up with emotion as he smiled affectionately at her.

'As ever, exactly when you said you'd arrive,' she teased him.

'I always stand by my word and, as ever,' he emphasised but not unkindly, 'you weren't ready.'

Carmen slid into the car, which as it had been imported from the UK, was a right hand drive.

'Always keep a man waiting,' she said impishly. 'That's what I was taught.'

He arched his eyebrows at her, then gently took the car down the drive.

***

Aaron was on a cruise through the streets of his manor, the part of London in which he operated. He was at the wheel of the BMW, the music blaring though the speakers, very much drawing attention to himself, which is what he intended.

Dean sat alongside, slowly mulling things over, as Aaron took a tour of gangland, the true scale of which remained unknown to most people even though the Metropolitan Police had publicly identified over 260 gangs, many based and operating from the postcode areas in which the members lived. Whilst a large number of the gangs simply postured, others were serious gangs involved in robbery and murder. Aaron's E2 gang was slowly being groomed by him to become a major player on the scene and this journey he was taking with Dean was akin to a dog pissing on its territory.

He chugged slowly around Haggerston Park, Hackney Road and Old Bethnal Green, checking for faces and possible unwanted incursions by other gangs, particularly the DNA Boys or the Hackney Posse, the two gangs representing the biggest threat to E2.

He was also on the lookout for graffiti that signalled possible war.

At one point he spotted an unknown face on Gossett Street, did a very dangerous U-turn and drew up alongside the youth who was loping idly along the road. Aaron kept up with him.

'Who you?' he demanded.

'Fuck wants to know?' the young lad shot back.

Aaron accelerated, bumped the car up onto the pavement and quickly jumped out, faced him. Dean was out, too, hovering just behind.

'I aks the question, I want the answer,' Aaron said. His right hand was down at his side and he turned it slightly so the intruder could see there was a blade in it.

'Hey, hey,' the lad said, backing off. 'I ain't here for no trouble.'

'So why are you here?'

'Just passin' through, man … no harm intended.' There was abject fear in his eyes as Aaron stepped up to him and placed the tip of the knife up to his neck. 'I see you again, boy, I cut your fuckin' eyes out.'

His head reared so he was looking down his nose and the lad turned and bolted much to Aaron's amusement.

Back in the car, on patrol, Aaron sensed that Dean was distracted by his thoughts.

'What's going on in that dumb head of yours?'

Dean shrugged. 'So, did you just talk?' he asked.

Aaron frowned, then realised what Dean was referring to. 'Fuck d'you want to know what me an' a bitch did?'

'Just … she … well…' Dean coughed uncomfortably.

Aaron thought he understood completely. 'Oh, man, you want sloppy seconds?'

'No, no,' Dean protested. 'I like Lauren, yeah, but if you…'

'Alright, we'll sort something.'

'If you're with Lauren now, bro, that's cool,' Dean said.

'Dickhead! I ain't with her … gotta keep my options open, innit?'

Dean was now confused and dismayed, whilst Aaron was relishing his verbal bullying tactics.

'Easy, yeah … be fuckin' funny to see you get laid, anyways,' Aaron chuntered. He fished out his phone, began texting with both hands as he steered the car with his knees.

***

Lauren still wasn't completely certain how she had been sucked into Aaron's world. She had first seen him in a KFC near Mile End Park where she'd ended up one night after going to the cinema with a couple of her friends. Aaron had been at a table at the far end of the restaurant with four of his friends, laughing, larking about and catching the eyes of the girls.

Lauren had caught him staring at her with serious intent and what she experienced from that was a mixture of powerful sexual excitement and a hint of danger.

He followed her out and trailed her like a puppy dog to Mile End tube station where, much to her friends' dismay, she told them to go while she talked to Aaron who she found to be funny and warm. When he tried to kiss her, she held back and he seemed to respect the fact she wasn't going to be easy and if anything happened between them it would only be after they got to know each other first.

'I totally get that,' he said sweetly. 'Catch up with ya.'

He left her standing there, mouth agape, not even knowing his last name.

And he had played her well, enticed her into his world – albeit on the periphery – introducing her to some of his friends, including Dean Walker who seemed much nicer, shyer, than the others and slightly out of place. But she was soon having a lot of fun, tear-arsing around in Aaron's shed of a BMW (that he loved), doing daft things until, eventually, she was the one to lead him to her bed.

That experience had not been as she had envisaged and she could not work out why. A huge part of her wanted it to end now, but another stronger, wilder part wanted it to go on because life with Aaron had really got under her skin, like some of the drugs she knew he sold, but which she had yet to experience. At least he hadn't tried to force anything like that on her. What he had done was romance her, play her, then screw her … yet, yet, yet … she wanted more, even if he treated her badly.

She was in her bedroom, sitting on the bed, legs crossed, knees drawn up, looking at herself in the full length mirror on the wall.

Her mascara had run because of her tears and she looked like a badger. She had been crying but the sobs had subsided and her breath was now coming in only minor judders as opposed to those that had been shaking her whole body.

'Oh God,' she moaned quietly, then jumped when he phone buzzed to announce the arrival of a text message.

She picked it up, looked at the screen and her heart began to pound.

It was from Aaron.

She held her breath as she read it. 'Soz bout earlier. Meat me @ 10 by Chkn Hut.'

Something akin to a rainbow enveloped her.

She gasped gratefully as she texted back, just as the front door opened and slammed shut and a woman's voice from downstairs called up. 'Hi Lauren, I'm home.'

'Hi mum,' she called back and leapt off the bed whilst wiping away the sadness from her face: it was on again. She and Aaron were going to be something. 'Us.'

***

Whilst the E-type was a brutal classic, rather like its owner, the suspension was dated and Richie's magnificent car rolled somewhat on the curves of the Spanish coastal road as he sped along, fast but not dangerously. Both he and Carmen were enjoying seeing the sun begin to dip huge and orange over the horizon, the citron colours seizing the sky.

Carmen was laughing, touching up her mascara to make certain it wasn't running as the warm breeze wafted into her face.

They were part-way through a conversation, Riche protesting about something Carmen had said.

'He's my brother, not royalty.'

'You asked me to arrange a party for his birthday and this is how we do things. Only the best in Espana.' She clicked her fingers as though she was a Flamenco dancer clacking castanets whilst keeping her smile on Richie.

'Carmen, thank you … it all sounds amazing … and expensive … I mean, really expensive…' Richie pressed his foot down at the next, tight bend, using sustained speed to keep the Jag from wallowing too much. He concentrated on this.

'I know how important Charlie is to you, so it has to be beyond amazing.'

Richie nodded, dropped a gear. The car surged beautifully.

'Plus,' Carmen added cheekily, 'if it wasn't amazing I wouldn't be able to charge quite so much money.'

Richie allowed himself a chuckle, changed up and hit the speed limit.

***

From his position in the tower block flat high above Bethnal Green, the north-easterly aspect from the balcony made Aaron feel as if he was master of all he surveyed. It wasn't quite true, but one day he hoped it would be. There were other tougher, better organised post code gangs out there and Aaron realised his supremacy in the area would not happen overnight. But happen it would. He was prepared to be tougher and better organised than anyone else.

One of the best ways he knew to achieve this was to be the leader the E2 gang both feared and respected, but who also met their needs. He had to look after the fuckers, too.

Like tonight.

By leaning out across the balcony rail from the flat and looking slightly south and west, Aaron could just see the top of the London Eye, the tip of Big Ben and ninety-three million miles beyond that, the setting sun … or at least he could have done if there wasn't so much dark cloud filling the sky and drizzle falling on another miserable evening in London town.

'Wank,' he said, pushing himself back off the railings.

The sliding door from the balcony into the flat was open and inside a few members of E2 were sprawling around on the furniture, listening to pounding urban music, smoking joints and ciggies and slamming back Jaeger-bombs.

Dean was out on the balcony with him, leaning thoughtfully on the rail, watching the lights of the city come on. He didn't notice Aaron slyly looking at him just a moment before the leader leaned into the flat and shouted, 'Who wants to get laid tonight?'

A chorus of excited 'Yesses' greeted the question. Every single one of them wanted to get laid.

Dean turned his head, frowning anxiously, his guts doing a tight flip. 'Is this about Lauren?'

Aaron's face became an expression of pure evil. 'Course. Slag needs some teaching.'

35

Dean was confused, then slightly hopeful. 'So you really don't want her?'

'You a real gem … I'm a generous leader, bud.' Aaron paused for the killer punchline. 'She's for everyone.'

If Aaron hadn't been standing right in front of him, Dean would have staggered backwards as his legs suddenly became rubbery with the horror of the implication. Aaron misread Dean's non-verbal reaction.

'What's this?' he asked him playfully. 'You scared of the bruvs seeing you do your ting with your ding?' He could not even begin to conceive that any member of the gang would not be up for what he was going to sort. He laughed dirtily, then went inside, leaving Dean alone on the balcony. He turned to the railings and gripped them tight, no longer able to focus on the view in front of him.

***

The restaurant was actually in one corner of a marina in which hundreds of high class, luxurious motor boats and yachts were moored. It was a place Richie loved, particularly at this time of day as the sun left the sky, the shadows grew long and he was with Carmen.

A waiter brought aperitifs. Carmen went to sip hers but paused, waiting for Richie as he stirred his straw anti-clockwise three times. She smiled. This was all very normal for her. Then they clinked glasses and sipped before she took out her mobile phone.

'You should call him, make sure he's sober enough to get onto the plane.'

He looked flatly at her. 'Carmen, he's not a drunk … I called the local earlier and he wasn't even in.'

'Honestly?'

'Honestly.'

'Okay, I tell you what, I'll call the Dover Castle and if he's not there, I'll buy you dinner.' She tabbed through her contacts menu, pressed call.

Mocking seriously, Richie said, 'As a client, I thought you were buying me dinner anyway.'

She kicked him gently under the table, smiled and turned away slightly as the call connected.

FOUR

1968: London: Hatton Gardens.

Back then they were young, reckless and unafraid. Unfortunately they were not the best of planners, but that was a skill they would learn from experience.

They had chosen the target, a jeweller's shop – of course – on Hatton Garden Street itself, London's jewellery quarter and the centre of the UK diamond trade. It should have been easy. From an informant they knew that on that particular day in June, there had been a delivery of diamonds to the value of just under £250,000, from which they could expect to see seventy grand once the diamonds were sold on to their fence.

In those days it was big money and worth the risk.

There were four of them – Richie and Charlie Archer, Del 'Butch' Kelly and Arthur Bennett. Two each on two scooters and they pulled up on Leather Lane, which runs parallel with Hatton Gardens, at 9.30 am that morning. Their information was that the diamonds would have been delivered to the shop at nine where they would be sorted and graded.

Kelly and Bennett were the scooter riders, Richie and Charlie the actual robbers.

On Leather Lane they made their final preparations.

Scarfs were pulled up and across their faces underneath their motorcycle helmets and the Archer brothers alighted from the back of the scooters, each armed with a sledgehammer.

There was going to be no subtlety here.

They were on the corner of the junction with Greville Street which runs across Hatton Gardens and the target shop was also on that corner.

They jogged at a crouch, dressed in bike leathers, twisted into Hatton Garden Street and then attacked the front doors of the shop with the sledgehammers, crashing the heavy tools down into the full length glass which shattered and as the brothers stepped through to terrorise the staff and demand the diamonds, their getaway riders drew up outside.

Charlie crossed to the main counter and smashed it to smithereens with one ferocious blow of his sledgehammer. The girl behind reared back, screaming and suitably terrified and Charlie screamed back at her, 'We want the fucking gems.'

At that moment the security door behind the counter opened and four men surged out, the owner and thee colleagues. The first through that door was armed with a fire extinguisher pointed at Charlie's face, which the man activated. A huge cloud of noxious foam hit Charlie. He staggered back, his eyes streaming as if he'd been laced with mustard gas. He dropped the sledgehammer on his foot, hobbled around in a circle screaming in agony as the extinguisher guy turned it to Richie and fired. At the same time, the three other men set about the brothers who valiantly fought them off as they retreated out of the shop and ran towards the waiting scooters.

Butch Kelly over-revved his machine at the same time as releasing the brake and engaging gear. It shot out uncontrollably from under him, did a three-sixty somersault and crashed back to each, only just missing Butch who threw himself out of the way.

Charlie pushed Richie out of his way and jumped astride Arthur's scooter, which he powered up, but as the back wheel hit a grate, the tyre lost its grip and fell sideways, hurling the robbers off as if they'd been thrown from a kids' roundabout.

The staff from the jewellery shop went after them, but realising the game was well and truly up, the four luckless robbers legged it ignominiously towards Holborn Viaduct, not one penny richer for their endeavours.

***

London: Present Day.

'But y'see, it was a learnin' curve for us lags ... one o' those things you put down to experience and move on. I'm just happy to say that me an' Richie and all the others were all part of the history of that very famous area of London … it was an honour.' Charlie Archer raised his glass to the small, attentive cluster of people around his table, listening to his story of the bungled heist not far from fifty years ago now, all laughing in all the right places.

'An' you never got fingered for it?' one of them asked.

'Nah,' Charlie said. 'Old Bill never came a-knocking.' He tapped his nose.

'What I don't get,' the same person asked, 'is why you didn't wear a full face helmet.'

'Cos,' – and here Charlie encouraged the group like the conductor of an orchestra and they all said in unison, 'they didn't exist in them days.' It was a well-practised moment. 'In fact, nothing existed back then and guess what?' Charlie asked them all. 'We didn't miss it. They were good days,' he concluded wistfully.

'What about retribution?' another of the group asked him.

Charlie's face clouded over, suddenly becoming serious. 'Retribution? What d'you mean by that?'

'Well, er,' the guy said uneasily, 'the people in the shop … y'know? The fire extinguisher and all that.'

Charlie caught the eye of one of the group. Her name was Lizzy Davies. She was a few years younger than Charlie, just in her sixties whereas he was almost leaving his. She looked forty and had a strong twinkle in her eye, but she too had a cloud of seriousness on her face at the question of retribution. Charlie gave her a smile.

'Nah,' he said. 'They were good. They had bottle and weren't afraid to protect themselves from a few jumped up dickheads like we were in those days. We left 'em alone … for a year anyway. Then we robbed the fuckers blind.'

Charlie's little audience burst into laughter, not really certain if the claim was true or not.

It was. As was the tale of non-retribution, although Charlie did fail to mention that their insider, the one who gave Richie and himself the gen on the diamonds but failed to mention the violent shop owners, was subjected to a very severe form of retribution. Charlie could still see his body floating away down Limehouse Reach on the Thames. That memory brought the flicker of a smile to his ageing lips.

Charlie Archer reached for his glass and sipped the wine, glancing around the pub, the Dover Castle. He remembered how it used to be, an East End old-school boozer, a place where he and Richie often came to lick their wounds and plan causing wounds on others. Times had changed for the pub, managers and brewers came and went and for a long time the place had been closed. New management had gutted it and tried to bring it bang up to date by serving gastro food on nice tables with a very posh décor. Although they tried, they were failing to bring in a new wave of clientele and the regulars remained the same, middle aged and older. People who wanted simplicity in their local.

That said, the atmosphere was jovial and non-threatening and that evening it centred mainly around one person who had been keeping half a dozen other souls entertained by his regaling of bungled heists in the sixties.

The phone on the bar rang and the landlord, Giles Mainwaring, who had also been earwigging the tales from behind the bar, scooped it up and answered it. Then he covered the speaker with his hand and said, 'Mr Archer?' He held up the phone, catching Charlie's eye. 'Phone for you.'

'Excuse me ladies and gents,' he said and rose from his seat, walking over and taking the phone from Giles's hand.

' 'ello,' he said gruffly.

At the other end of the line, twelve hundred miles away, Carmen gestured an 'I told you so,' to Richie. Fancy finding Charlie in the boozer after all.

Richie shrugged good natured defeat.

'Mr Archer,' she said to Charlie, 'please hold the line for your brother, Mr Archer.' Carmen handed Richie her phone.

'Charlie, my boy,' Richie said.

'You don't even dial your own phone calls now? Fucking show-off!'

Richie ignored this. 'And you just happened to be passing the pub, right?'

'Pub?' Charlie looked despairingly around the Dover Castle. 'Things keep changing around here, Richie boy. Now it's more of a restaurant that lets you have a drink,' – he shot a terrifying stare at Giles – 'if you're lucky.' Charlie dragged one of the laminated menus towards him. 'And I quote ... special of the day ... Pigeon Breast Fritter, what's a fuckin' pigeon breast fritter for fuck's sake? With beetroot chutney ... Jeez.'

This time he gave Giles an amused glance. The landlord responded with an apologetic shrug.

In Spain, Richie smiled as he imagined his brother's dismay.

'People actually eat pigeons now ... probably because there's so many of them,' Charlie said.

'And that's why I'm here in a restaurant with a view of the Mediterranean, eating the freshest fish possible,' Richie said.

'I can tell you miss home,' Charlie said sarcastically.

The words struck a chord with Richie because, deep down, he did miss the place.

'You will come back one day, won't you little brother?' Charlie asked.

'You know my life is here now. There's nothing but trouble for me back there, Charlie.'

Charlie glanced across to the group of people he'd been chatting to, his eyes settling on Lizzy Davies as she touched her hair back over her ear. Charlie could easily visualise her thirty years younger. She laughed, tilting her head, looking radiant.

'Oh, I don't know about nothing,' Charlie said mysteriously.

Richie moved the subject on. 'Charlie, I'm really looking forward to seeing you.'

'You too, brother.'

'Good ... so take a hint, go home and get your head down. You're not as young as you used to be.'

'And neither are you, you cheeky sod.'

'Do NOT miss the flight ... I'll be at the airport waiting for you.'

'Over my dead body.'

They both hung up, smiling and excited by the prospect of seeing each other again. It had been too long.

Charlie handed the phone back to Giles then returned to his table where the numbers had thinned considerably, now only Lizzy there. He sat beside her and reached for his drink.

'Well, my kid brother has just told me to get home.'

Lizzy blinked and realised what he meant ... Richie. She retained her composure though and said casually, 'Him telling you what to do. How times change.'

'They do, darling Lizzy – and not always for the best.'

Lizzy's throat had gone a little bit dry at the thought of Richie. 'How is he?' she asked tentatively. 'Richie?' She almost whispered the name.

'Same old, same old ... you know him.'

'I ain't seen him for ... God, twenty-odd years, maybe more. I had a proper thing for him when he was younger,' she confessed pensively.

Charlie reacted, mock-hurt. 'Oi, what about me?'

'You're too old for me.' She laughed, but Charlie pretended to be sad. 'But you're still a looker, though.'

He gave a short laugh and shook his head. He pulled out a small note book, scribbled a number on a blank page and tore it out, handing it to Lizzy.

'Here's Richie's number if you ever want to speak to him.' He raised his eyebrows.

She looked at the number. 'I'd be too scared.'

'Scared? The guy's a pussy cat these days, but if you're scared, fine.' He held open his arms. 'Fancy coming home with me instead?' It was time for his eyes to twinkle suggestively.

'I wouldn't know what to do with it after all these years,' she admitted.

'That I don't believe.' He smiled, stood up and slid into his jacket. Gallantly he took Lizzy's hand and kissed it. 'Good night, sweet princess.'

***

'That was good, yeah?' Aaron said. His warm smile seemed to have an effect on Lauren that she could not quite understand. It really did make her weak at the knees and somehow, when he looked at her this way, it was as if she was the only person in the world to him and everything centred on her. God, she thought, he could really turn it on and when he does I just can't help myself. He reached across the table and touched a strand of her hair out of her eyes, one of those intimate gestures that true lovers made; small but very, very significant. 'You got beautiful eyes, babe,' he told her.

'Thank you,' she said.

'Y'know ... y'know ... about before ... I didn't mean those words, those hurtful words ... they was, I guess...' He dropped his eye line shyly. 'I was just nervous around you, y'know, that effect you have on me ... I go to pieces, y'know...'

'Me too,' she whispered throatily.

They were in the Chicken Hut near Mile End Park and he had treated them both to a chicken burger and Fanta orange.

Aaron checked his big bling watch and if Lauren had been a better reader of body language and not so gullible she would have seen the flicker of something cross Aaron's face as his eyes narrowed and would have been on her guard.

'What now?' she asked, touching the back of his hand with a fingertip.

'Something special ... you up for something special?'

'With you, yeah.'

'Come on.' He took her hand and led her out of the restaurant onto the street where they walked side by side, hand in hand.

Without warning, Aaron pulled her skilfully into his arms and kissed her, but as she groaned and responded, he took hold of her arms firmly and led her into an alleyway. She went willingly, certain that a moment of romance was about to unfold, but as Aaron walked her down the centre of the alley, there was movement in the shadows.

Lauren emitted a squeak, clutched Aaron's forearm.

He laughed.

Then there was more movement and the whites of eyes caught in reflections from a flickering lamp post and the black shadows came to life as members of the E2 gang materialized like a horde of demons. Aaron pushed her towards them and they started to circle her.

'What's going on?' she asked, her head jerking back and forth, trying to keep track on the gang.

'Well,' Aaron shrugged, 'aren't you supposed to introduce new girlfriends to your family? I'm an old fashioned guy … meet my family, bitch.'

There was a low repetitive chant emanating from the gang. 'E2, E2, E2…'

***

Charlie Archer emerged from the Dover Castle and inhaled the London night air deep into his chest, which after fifteen years of (almost) non-smoking felt as if he could breathe in the whole of the city.

The 'almost' was that he allowed himself one ciggie per night and only one. He'd had a scare with his lungs and learned a harsh lesson but although the treatment had been successful he still needed just a few drags to quell the longing to smoke that never quite went away.

He selected a cigarette from his diamond encrusted case, closed it, tapped the end and lit it up, smiling as he drew in the smoke, thinking about Richie and Lizzy and wondering why the hell the two of them hadn't got it together all those years before. They would have been good for each other, but events happened, lives changed routes, and it was not to be. He half-wondered about getting her on the plane to Spain with him tomorrow and surprising Richie, but it was probably too late to arrange that now … practically and emotionally.

He shrugged. Richie's love life had always been a tangled mess and Charlie had always made a point of keeping well out of it, so he wasn't going to poke his nose in at this late stage of the game. He walked on, took one last pull on the cigarette and crushed it out.

He walked along confidently. He might have been knocking on the door of seventy, but he still strode upright and tall, barrel chested and cocky. If he required it, people still gave him a wide berth, but it was a rare request these days.

He passed the front door of Chicken Hut on Tent Street, his nose screwing up at the fat-filled odour emanating from the establishment, continuing on past a few alleyways until he stopped suddenly, thinking he had heard something which in his parlance, he would call 'untoward'. A yelp, a muffled scream, voices, cruel laughter. He peered into the alley, thinking, 'Kids just mucking around.'

Charlie became tense when he heard another yelp. This time it was the cry of a female and Charlie could distinguish between the sound of fun and the sound of terror. This was the latter. A strange sensation filtered down to the tips of his fingers and he turned into the alley without hesitation.

***

JP's hand was plastered over Lauren's mouth, muting her words and cries, as other E2 members tried to haul her face down over a wheelie bin, but she was struggling like a captured leopardess, though this fight seemed to be whooping E2 into a frenzy of excitement.

None of them could see the expression on Dean Walker's face who had gathered in the alley with the other gang members on Aaron's orders, all waiting expectantly for him to appear.

Some clearly knew why they were here but none would tell Dean, though he knew it was something to do with Lauren.

If he was honest with himself, deep down he knew – and it horrified him.

Then Aaron and Lauren had arrived, she was encircled and now she was pinned over the bin, JP's hand smothering her face and three others holding her squirming body, exposing the top of her legs underneath her short skirt. A couple of gang members were recording the proceedings on their smartphones.

Dean tried to make his way to Lauren but, misinterpreting his actions, Leroy and couple of gang members blocked his path.

'Ah, ah, ah … wait to be invited to get your cock out, Dean, you horny monster,' Leroy warned him.

Aaron watched the interaction through slitted eyes and said, 'Okay, come on Dean … time to lose your cherry.'

Dean hesitated, unsure, seeing something vile in Aaron who strode over to him, grabbed his tee shirt front and pulled him close to Lauren. 'Pull her fucking skirt up and shove your cock up her arse … get on wiv it,' Aaron shouted, his spittle flying.

'Oi – what's going on?'

Charlie appeared in the alley, striding towards the gang. They turned, pocketed the smartphones quickly.

Aaron stood boldly between Charlie and what was happening. 'Fuck off, grandpa, this has got jack-shit to do with you,' he told him.

Charlie stepped sideways for a better view and as he fully realised what grim hell he had stepped into, his eyes became cold and ferocious, his teeth clenched in a wolf-like snarl.

They were holding Lauren rigid over the bin, her skirt yanked right up exposing her scanty panties and the clear intention of the gang: rape.

But then JP screamed as Lauren bit him deep in the fleshy part of his hand between thumb and forefinger, her sharp young teeth sinking in and drawing blood from the rubbery chunk of meat.

JP managed to keep her pressed down, and he raised his fist high about to smash it into the side of her face. Her eyes saw what was about to happen and she braced herself for the blow.

Charlie intervened. 'I really, really, really wouldn't do that.' JP's fist hovered in mid-air, hesitating because of the threatening timbre of Charlie's authoritative voice.

Another E2 spoke up. 'You been told to fuck off, old man.'

Unintimidated – and actually feeling a rush of excitement – Charlie declared, 'I'm warning you all now. Anyone tells me to fuck off one more time and they won't have a jaw left after I've…'

The E2 reiterated: 'Fuck off.'

Charlie seemed to grow, literally rising to the occasion, as he slowly pulled his right hand out of his pocket, his four fingers having threaded into his knuckleduster, a little piece of equipment that he had inherited from his father who had taken it from a soldier following a brawl in an East End boozer on

VE day. His father, incidentally, had not taken any active part in the war effort other than by buying and selling goods on the black market and making a very tidy sum for himself. Charlie carried the knuckleduster as a memento, never expecting to have to use it again.

Pulling it out was the only slow part. Very much like the old weapon, Charlie was a bit rusty but still deadly and in spite of his age, very fast when wound up.

Charlie smashed the E2 youth in the face.

The knuckleduster did its job, concentrating the force of the punch by directing it towards a smaller contact area with the result that there was increased tissue damage and the likelihood of fracturing bone. At the same time, the extended palm grip absorbed the counter force from the blow which could have otherwise damaged Charlie's own hand. Without a knuckleduster, there was every possibility of breaking your own hand on the victim's face.

It worked as intended.

Charlie felt the satisfying crack as the blow broke the E2's jaw and dislocated it at the same time, knocking the lad's face unnaturally out of shape. He went down instantly, spitting out blood and teeth, but also so disorientated from the shockwave of the blow through his brain that he had no conception whatsoever what had just happened to him. Just that it hurt and he had been injured badly.

'What the fuck?' said JP, stunned like everyone by the speed, ferocity and unexpectedness of the assault.

For fuck's sake, this was on old man.

Legs shoulder width apart, almost adopting a boxer's stance, Charlie said, 'About time someone taught you filth a lesson.'

Then Aaron stepped into the fray, using calming gestures to his gang who were bristling. 'You just fucked up,' he informed Charlie.

'No, you did,' Charlie said, unafraid.

Aaron shook his head. 'I don't think so.'

Charlie could see and sense that Aaron was the gang leader. 'Come on then, you and me.'

Aaron shook his head, laughing in disbelief. 'That's not how it happens these days, old man.' He gave a 'follow me' gesture to the gang and said, 'Boys.'

The gang member still holding Lauren over the bin threw her to one side and stepped towards Charlie with the other E2s, forming a semi-circle with Aaron at the centre of the arc.

Lauren stumbled away, her clothing in disarray, only just keeping her footing, catching Dean's eyes as she backed up against the wall, seeing the shame on his face and the little boy lost look, a young lad who had found himself embroiled in a situation he did not want to be part of. He stood isolated from the gang that was now tightening its formation and edging towards Charlie. Aaron was central, Maz, JP and Leroy flanking him.

'What?' Charlie's voice was full of disbelief. 'You can't do anything one–to-one?'

'That's how it is, granddad,' Aaron confirmed.

'You know what you are?'

'What would that be?'

'A fucking coward,' Charlie said.

Aaron gave a 'whatever' shrug and sucked in through his teeth.

Charlie shook his head. 'I gotta say I hate it when you lot do that,' but his eyes flicked left, right, scanning the ranks of the gang. There were a lot of them.

Suddenly Maz lunged at him, his knife slashing, the knife he had used to stab the eyes out of the children's faces in the photograph in the flat that the gang had trashed.

He sliced at Charlie, who raised his arm defensively. Maz whipped the razor sharp blade across the forearm, cutting through Charlie's jacket sleeve and his flesh. Charlie fell back, clutching the wound and that slight retreat was the signal on which the gang descended on him like hyenas attacking a wounded lion. It was at this moment that Lauren fled.

They rained punches, kicks and knife slashes on him.

He could not turn quickly enough now to defend himself from all the angles and eventually he went down onto his knees as the ferocity increased, but he fought back as best he could.

Aaron actually stood back and watched with pride and amusement, his hands on his hips like a pitch-side football coach watching his team massacre the opposition, nodding, using words of encouragement, his head bobbing. Then he took out his smartphone and began filming.

Dean took no part, creeping back into the shadows, nauseated.

'Yo, man, hold this,' Aaron ordered JP and handed him the phone before wading in and hauling his gang out of the way, like a dog digging for a bone.

Charlie, battered and bleeding, was on the cold hard ground, covered in slash wounds, cuts, bruises, his face a horrific mess. He gasped for breath, the lungs that had only minutes before felt fresh and healthy struggling to draw in air. They now sounded as though they were being operated by an iron lung, making a wheezing noise like a set of bellows.

Aaron towered over him. 'You wanted one-on-one, old man? C'mon, get up, fight me.' He jiggled his fingers, trying to entice Charlie up, knowing that victory was his.

Charlie drew on his last reserves as he tried to push himself up. 'About time you got your hands dirty, you coward,' he gasped and spat out a chunk of broken, bloody tooth. It was slow and agonising, but Charlie forced himself up onto his knees, his age proving no barrier to his innate determination and he still had more courage left in his heart than all of E2 put together.

As he got his balance, primitive fury overtook Aaron – coupled with the fear that if Charlie was allowed to get to his feet, he might just have enough reserves in him to seriously embarrass Aaron.

A kick lashed out, a flat-footed smack on the side of Charlie's head, sending him sprawling.

Charlie writhed.

Aaron came alongside, sneering, and before Charlie could even begin to recover, Aaron growled, 'One-on-one? You got it.'

He stamped on Charlie's head. It felt good under his foot.

'Get the fucker,' an E2 voice encouraged him.

'Yeah, get him,' said another.'

'E2 … E2 … E2,' a low chant began.

Aaron rose to his full height, egging them on, and then to the beat of the chant he began to stomp on Charlie's head, again and again, as a terrible almost insatiable rage overcame him. He pounded Charlie's head, feeling the skull break, feeling the jaw snap, feeling the cheekbones break like twigs, feeling the nose crumble … until the supportive baying of the gang fell to silence as Aaron continued the frenzied assault just to the beat of what was drumming in his own head until he ran out of energy and stopped.

Then, apart from Aaron's own heavy breathing, there was silence.

The smartphones were pocketed and the gang realised they had witnessed something very, very terrible.

Aaron looked around at everyone, seeing their stunned faces, his survey stopping on JP. The two eyed each other.

A pulse, then JP said, 'Respect for ya, blud,' and the moments of tension were released.

JP fist-bumped Aaron, the gesture of victory, and once more pack mentality overtook them as they all fought to backslap and fist-bump and high-five Aaron, as well as each other. Aaron basked in the glory of taking his pack to another level, one much murkier and more dangerous than even he could have conceived.

He took a bow, then pointed at the E2 member that Charlie had flattened. He was still on the ground, semi-conscious, groaning, his limbs moving slowly. 'Get that pussy out of here,' he ordered.

Charlie's eyes were unfocused, hazy, their viewpoint literally at street level. It is claimed that vision, followed by hearing are the last two senses to go prior to death. Charlie saw the legs of the gang through steamed up eyes and the last words he ever heard spoken came from Aaron's foul mouth.

'Sill old fuckwit.'

***

Lizzy ordered another glass of wine when Charlie left her in the Dover Castle then she moved to an empty seat at the back of the pub to sip it and reflect for a few minutes on the enigma that was Richie Archer, bad boy gangster who she had somehow let slip through her fingers all those years ago. It had been one of those situations where, perhaps, two people who should have been together were never free at the same time; one was in a relationship, the other not, then vice versa.

She gave a short, sad laugh as she thought about it.

'Now that he even knew,' she said to herself. 'I really am a stupid…'

She tipped back the remainder of the wine, collected herself and her things together, gave Giles and a couple of the other regulars a wave, blew kisses, then left the pub.

She was approaching the entrance to the alleyway just beyond the Chicken Hut as the E2 gang emerged. They were talking animatedly but her presence seemed to mute them for a moment as they filed past, glaring at her as she stood resolute on the footpath, holding her ground and making them go around her. One purposely shoulder-barged her, trying to knock her off balance.

'Oi you little fucker, show some respect,' she said.

The whole gang stopped and turned menacingly to stare at her.

She thought they smelled of something pungent, but wasn't sure what. Her nose screwed up.

Then the biggest, hardest looking one of them stepped up to her.

She glared at him boldly.

He made the shape of a pistol with his hand, pointing the two fingers of the barrel at her, forefinger, middle finger, thumb cocked back like a trigger, the palm of his hand parallel to the ground. He pulled his thumb back, made a clicking sound, then said, 'Bang,' softly.

Passers-by on the opposite side of the street scurried on.

The big lad blew across his fingertips as though he was blowing smoke from the muzzle of a fired gun, turned on his heels and headed off into the night, the gang clustered around him.

'Little shits,' Lizzy said. She walked on, glanced down the alleyway, then stopped, not sure if she had seen anything.

With caution she approached a shape on the ground that became clearer the closer she got to it.

Charlie sprawled out in a way that could only mean one thing: he was dead. She stifled a scream, ran back to the end of the alley, but there was no sign of the gang. She rooted out her phone from her bag and dialled 999.

'Police please,' she said, her voice dithering, 'yes, it's a fucking emergency.'

FIVE

Even as DI Susan Taylor ordered the second pint of Stella – this one with a whisky chaser – she knew she was doing the wrong thing. The double whisky that followed served to confirm this: she was being an arse. She was only glad that she made it home without seeing a cop car and that the house was in darkness. What an ignominy it would have been to get breathalysed, even though she thought she would be under the limit … just.

As she undressed in the darkened en-suite bathroom, clattering around, dropping the toilet seat, knocking over the toothpaste, she knew she was moving like an elephant and as she slid into the huge double bed and tugged the duvet up to her throat, she hoped to God there wasn't a call-out because she knew that boozing whilst on the rota was a big no-no.

She fell asleep instantly.

She didn't know for how long or how many times the phone had been ringing.

For a while it was a sound that mixed with her dark dreams, but then she shot upright, knocked the bedside light off the cabinet and fumbled for her mobile.

Her voice sounded thick in her throat. 'Yuh?'

'Guv? Where've you been? I've been calling you forever,' DC Graham Watts whined.

She closed her eyes, swallowed something unpleasant and rubbed her face with her free hand. Her skin felt like sharkskin … looked smooth, but felt harsh.

'What time is it?'

'Just after three.'

'What's going on?' She was still half in another place and her mouth felt and tasted like the entrance to the underworld. Maybe she'd had more whisky than she remembered.

'We got one, Guv,' Watts said.

Why the fuck did he have to sound so fucking lively, she thought crossly.

'Gimme details.' She rose out of bed, accidentally pulled the duvet off. Automatically, not thinking, she turned and said, 'Sorry love,' but then stopped herself because there was no one to apologise to. She screwed up her face, held back the tears. She found her pad and pen on the floor, righted the lamp and knelt in front of the bedside cabinet as if it was a shrine. She scribbled notes that looked incomprehensible as Watts outlined the situation: body ... bad assault ... old guy ... alleyway ... Chicken Hut.

'Have I got time for a shower?' she asked Watts.

'Depends on how glam you think you need to look at a murder scene,' Watts said cheekily.

'I need to look as good as Angie Dickinson...'

'Who? Is that the DI over in Streatham?'

Taylor could imagine the look of confusion on Watts' face. 'Before your time.'

She hung up, took a breath and straightened the bed. Then she leaned over to the far side of it and gently kissed the unused pillow and whispered, 'Duty calls, babe.'

She dived into the shower and eight minutes after that she was on the road.

***

The alleyway had been cordoned off at both ends and the full length of it was being treated as a crime scene.

The circus had moved in. Crime Scene Investigators were on site, a Home Office pathologist was en route, uniformed cops were being deployed in various capacities; a mobile generator and lighting rig had been set up, bathing the alley in bright, unforgiving light. For the moment, the body had been hidden from view by means of a collapsible barrier rather like a wind-break which would later be replaced by a crime scene tent which was on its way.

Taylor was issued with a billowing forensic suit from the back of the CSI van and was standing propped against the alley wall, fitting elasticated slippers over her shoes when

Watts, similarly dressed, came and stood in front of her as she stood upright.

'Mornin' Guv,' he said brightly.

She scowled at him. 'Fuck off being so … so bouncy. You're like Tigger.'

Watts grinned.

'What have we got? Can I have a look, yet?'

'Yeah … CSI and forensics have done the basics, so we can have a proper shuftie now, see if there's any actual ID on the guy.'

'Okay.'

Watts set off, but Taylor didn't move. He had gone ten feet before realising she wasn't with him. He stopped, turned. 'Guv?'

'Just getting my bearings,' she explained. 'I like to take my time when I walk up to a serious crime scene … you don't get a second chance, y'know?'

Watts understood, though he was more of a 'let's go and look now' type of detective. He knew Taylor liked to get the real feel of a crime scene, sniff it in, look at it from every angle.

It was fifteen minutes before Taylor actually stepped behind the barrier and looked at the body. She caught her breath. Behind her, Watts said, 'Not nice.'

'What an ugly way to die,' she commented, lowering herself onto her haunches about three feet away from the old man's battered, crushed, misshapen head. She angled her head to inspect his features, seeing how the blood had flowed from his mouth, nose and ears. Then she frowned.

'What did the witness say this man was called?'

'Charlie Archer,' Watts said.

'Oooh … not that I'm one to make predictions, but I think we might have our hands full with this one.'

***

The interview room was sparsely furnished. The table screwed to the floor, the tape recorder screwed to the table. The only decorations on the walls were notices about prisoners' rights,

CrimeStoppers, a couple of wanted posters and an ejaculating cock and balls some wag (probably a cop) had managed to draw in felt tip. The chairs were those ubiquitous ones with curved, hard plastic seats and tubular metal legs. Uncomfortable at the best of times. This was how the room had to be, sterile and as safe as possible.

The tape was running even though this was not a suspect interview, the witness having given permission for this.

Lizzy Davies was nursing a mug of tea, now cold, in the grip of her fingers. She looked shell-shocked, exhausted and had visibly aged with the events of the night.

Taylor had treated her gently but could see that Lizzy was brittle and could easily snap at any time.

What she had stumbled across had shaken her to her very core.

The interview was part way through and certain things had been established: the evening in the pub, the victim leaving; Lizzy having another drink, then setting off to walk home; the unruly gang emerging from the alleyway, Lizzy's slight confrontation with them, then the discovery of the body. Lizzy had already provided a witness statement to a uniformed constable, which included a description of the gang and her belief it was the E2 which controlled the streets in that area, a belief that came from her local knowledge.

It was late now and Lizzy had been at the police station almost all night. She was tired, irritable and had been just about to go, but the two detectives had collared her and she had reluctantly agreed to be spoken to again, even though her brain was all mush and all she wanted to do was cry.

'And how did you know the deceased?' Taylor asked Lizzy,.

'The same way everyone in this neighbourhood knows,' – she corrected herself with a gulp – 'knew him.'

'I see,' Taylor said, understanding.

Watts, however, did not. 'And how is that?' he asked curtly. 'How did everyone know him?'

Lizzy frowned as she regarded Watts with disbelief. 'You've never heard of Charlie and Richie Archer?'

Watts pouted, shrugged and shook his head as if to say, 'Why should I?'

Taylor's bottom lip sagged incredulously because, clearly, she had heard of him.

'You one of those special coppers, the ones who work part time for free?' Lizzy asked scathingly.

Taken aback, Watts stuttered, 'I, well, no … I'm a detective constable.'

Lizzy huffed. 'I'd lose the word 'detective' … and the 'able' for that matter.'

Watts was still working that one out when Taylor snapped at him, 'Have you heard about the Kray twins? The Richardsons?'

'Yeah, course, the Krays. I even saw a film about them, but the actors weren't twins, which I thought…'

Taylor cut in, 'Well Charlie Archer was like them.'

Lizzy added, pointing to the floor, 'And this was Charlie and Richie's manor.'

'Oh, okay, I get it,' Watts said under pressure from the females. 'So they ran the place, took a slice of it.'

'Literally in some cases,' Taylor commented off the cuff.

Lizzy glared at her. 'You can mock, DI Taylor, but at least you could walk the streets without being harassed, or worse. What happened tonight is a disgrace. A single man murdered by a…'

'These days we try our best, but…' Taylor cut in.

'Yeah, yeah, I know you've had your budget cuts … I can't even remember the last time I saw coppers walking the beat at night, or day, come to that.' Lizzy began to get into her stride.

'Mrs Davies,' Watts interrupted.

She turned to him, her eyes blazing. 'It's Miss Davies,' she corrected him. 'If you'd bothered to read my statement which is in front of you, you'd have seen that, Detective Constable.'

Suitably chastened – he had only skimmed through the statement – Watts asked, 'You were saying Charlie Archer was murdered and seemed to be about to suggest something … did you see the murder?'

'I did not see the murder.' Lizzy shook her head. 'But I know it was that E2 gang.'

'What makes you say that?' Taylor asked.

'I recognised some of them. Not saying I know their names … they're like cockroaches scuttling around the streets. They need to be destroyed,' she concluded vehemently.

Watts sighed patronisingly. 'Miss Davies, it would be best if you didn't say things like that.'

'Why? They're destroying our community, our area, our way of life. And you want to protect them?'

'We do need evidence before we can do anything,' Taylor said.

'And what evidence are you likely to get from Charlie's murder scene? Fingerprints? CCTV? A murder weapon? Strong leads? Anything, for Christ's sake?' Lizzy clamped her mouth shut. She knew she was losing her equilibrium.

An uncomfortable silence descended on the room. The tape machine whirred. There was a voice somewhere down in the cells.

Taylor leaned forwards and asked, 'Did you see anyone causing Charlie Archer any harm? Did you see anyone murder him?'

Lizzy held Taylor's gaze. 'I know it was them. It doesn't take Sherlock to work that out … and back in the day, this sort of thing…'

'We don't live back in the day, Miss Davies, but I will follow up on your assumption that this E2 gang are connected and I will question them.'

Well that fills me with confidence,' Lizzy said in a tone which was the exact opposite. 'Can I go now?' She put her mug of cold tea on the table. 'I'm tired, upset and…'

'And what?' Taylor asked.

'And I hope you stand by your words,' she challenged Taylor. 'A good man died tonight.'

***

Watts came back into the interview room after escorting Lizzy out of the police station and arranging a lift home for her in a police car.

Taylor watched him sit, her fingers interlocked across her stomach.

'Technically not a good man,' she said.

Watts waited.

'He committed arson, theft, robbery and murder.' She blew out long and hard, her mouth still arid from her earlier alcohol intake.

'What happened to the brother?' Watts asked. 'Executed gangland style in a hail of bullets, no doubt?'

'No. Richie Archer … he fled, evaded the law … Spain.'

'Why?'

'Trust me, it was a good thing he did. Back in the day,' – Taylor smirked at her own use of this phrase, – 'Richie Archer was an unstoppable force. Unlike these postcode gangs, he left out the innocent, those not involved, but if you crossed him, even if you dared to question anything he said, that was it.' She cut her hand across her throat.

'Why have I never heard of him?'

Taylor looked at him, her face serious. 'Because anyone that knew him is too scared to talk…'

SIX

He had seen the dusk and now he was up to see the dawn and once again he was awed by the wonder of the universe.

Richie Archer poured a coffee from his cafetiere into his favourite mug and walked onto the upper balcony of his villa, the one on the east-facing side of the building that, if it had been in London, would have been called a gable-end.

But gable-ends were for terraced houses and post-war semis, not plush villas in Southern Spain.

He triple-sipped the coffee, then walked back inside the villa, trotted downstairs to the rear dining room where his collection of safes were on display, all nine of them: three, three and three.

He sat down and wondered which one he would chose to work on this morning.

***

It was pointless going to bed. There was far too much to do in terms of scene management and some fast track enquiries, and anyway, as Susan Taylor sipped her third cup of coffee, there was no way she could have got back to sleep anyway. The alcohol in her system had been replaced by caffeine, tiredness replaced by energy and she was buzzing … not necessarily functioning, but buzzing.

She had, hopefully, sorted the scene.

The CSI's had done their preliminary work before the Home Office pathologist arrived to examine the body in situ. That had happened even before she had landed. Then the body had been removed to the local public mortuary whilst even more detailed work was carried out at the scene by forensics and a fingertip search team.

Back in her office, Taylor had a notebook in front of her, trying to marshal her thoughts and put a few hypotheses together.

At the top of the page she had written, 'Why + when + where + how = who'.

It was the most simple problem solving approach, but despite that, it worked as a strategy for most murder investigations.

The she wrote, 'Victim/Location/Offender/Homicide.'

Under 'Victim' she wrote, 'Find out how he lived, find out how/why he died.'

Under 'Offender' she wrote 'E2', then a series of question marks.

Then she sipped her coffee some more because now, seriously, her head was hurting.

'Fuck,' she breathed and rubbed two very gritty eyes. 'Not functioning,' she said, 'not functioning.'

***

Lizzy paced the living room of her small house, a glass of whisky in her shaky hand, nervously sipping it as she went back and forth.

Eventually she stopped by the phone, pulled a scrap of paper out of her purse and unfolded it.

She took a steadying breath, then began to dial a number that started with the international dialling code 0034…

***

Richie was on his knees working on one of the locked safes. This was one that required total concentration and he was listening intently through his headphones to the inner workings of the safe as he slowly turned the dial, heard tumblers fall. This one was much thicker than the previous one and the villa had to be silent and he did not even dare breathe as his fingertips turned the dial so, so, so slowly. There was an almost imperceptible inner 'clunk' and Richie allowed himself a half-grin, then a blink of the eye as a bead of sweat dribbled down his forehead onto his eyelid.

One down, three to go.

The ringing of the telephone actually made him start – and his concentration was gone. He ripped the headphones off, swiped up the phone and gave a curt, 'Yes?'

'Mr Archer?'

He set his jaw. 'This better not be one of those bloody sales calls or whatever, especially at this time of day.'

'No, no … it's Lizzy Davies … you won't remember me, but…'

Richie got to his feet and started to walk out towards the pool, the phone cord stretching out behind him. 'Lizzy Davies?' he said.

In London, Lizzy held her breath.

'Lizzy Davies, 237 Torrance Street…' He smiled at the memory. 'Slim … long brown hair … lovely brown eyes.'

In London Lizzy squirmed and despite herself, her age and the reason she was making the call, a hot rush of excitement flooded through her lower belly, something she had not experienced for a long time. His voice, his memory had that effect on her.

'Oh I can't believe you remember me,' she said girlishly.

'I remember everyone,' Richie said, and that pricked her bubble somewhat – to realise she was just one of many to him.

'Oh,' she said, unable to hide the disappointment in that little word.

There was a beat of silence as Richie visualised the pretty girl he had once fancied like mad but who was way out on the very edge of his world.

Both waited for the other to speak.

'Hello?' Richie said, wondering if the connection was lost.

Lizzy composed herself. No more dreams now, back to reality. 'Mr Archer…'

'Call me Richie.' His voice had softened in his few moments of nostalgia and he smiled that 'one that got away' smile. Then he had a thought. 'How did you get my number, Lizzy? It's not exactly in the public domain, if you know what I mean?'

Lizzy gulped dryly and faltered as she said, 'Well, erm, I have some bad news … terrible news, in fact.'

Richie frowned. 'I haven't seen or heard from you in, how many years, and then you call me out of the blue on a number I don't just give to anyone and it's with terrible news. I really don't like the sound of this.'

Silence.

Lizzy was now too petrified to speak.

Richie waited, but when nothing was heard, he said, 'Lizzy? Are you still there?'

'Yes,' she squeaked thinly.

'I can sense you're upset or scared, my darling,' he said perceptively, 'but there's no reason to be. I've not been 'the person' you knew and remember for many years.'

'I … fine … I just…'

'Trust me, I'm a man of my word.'

'I … everyone … knew … knows that about you … it's one of the things I always liked about you.'

After a moment, Richie said, 'So, that's sorted out … now then, Lizzy Davies, why are you calling me at this time of day after all these years?'

'It's about Charlie … he gave me your number.'

And Lizzy began to tell Richie Archer about the sudden, brutal death of his beloved brother. The pleasant evening in the Dover Castle, Charlie setting off home, then later, herself walking home and discovering his badly beaten body in an alleyway and the immediate realisation that he was dead, murdered.

Charlie took it in, keeping logical and cool at first. Asking emotionless questions, trying to get his head around the enormity of what Lizzy was telling him, just trying to comprehend the sequence of events that had left his brother lying dead in a dirty alleyway.

He put the phone down then.

No histrionics. That had never been his thing. He had always reacted coldly to everything put before him. Initially.

He picked the phone up. There was only the ringing tone to hear.

He put the phone down.

Always, always, he took things without blowing up there and then.

He picked up the phone, put it down, picked it up, put it down.

Then he walked inside and went to the drinks cabinet, opened it, closed it, three times, then took out a bottle of Johnny Walker and a glass, pouring the golden liquid into it three times until it overflowed.

Something had started to bubble inside his chest, and he started to crumble. In his hand, the whisky glass shook as he raised it to his lips and took three sips before throwing it against the wall and smashing it.

The rage had begun.

***

They were on a skate park at the north tip of Mile End Park, the Regents Canal running along one side of it, Grove Road the other. They dominated it, acting as though they owned the concrete curves and loops, intimidating any other kids that might want to play, innocently, there.

'Devastated by bombing in World War Two,' Susan Taylor mused outloud as she watched the E2 gang on the skate park. She was in the driver's seat of her car, Graham Watts sitting alongside her and although Watts was also watching the youths, his eyes kept dropping slyly to Taylor's legs as her skirt rose up unintentionally above her knees. He thought she had very nice pins and it was all he could do not to touch them. His nostrils flared.

He swallowed and said, 'What?' croakily.

'Bombs, World War Two,' she repeated. 'Not only that, the sixty thousand Men of Essex camped here and met Richard the Second in 1381, I think it was, during the Peasants' Revolt. There have been plans to make a park here since the end of the war, but it's only really in the last ten years or so that any real development has taken place.'

'Oh, right.'

'Am I boring you?'

'Well … history,' he said weakly. 'Not my strong point.'

'You should be interested,' she chastised him. 'History is what makes us who we are, what we are today.'

'Ok, Guv.'

Lecture over, they turned back to look at E2. Aaron, Dean and DK were dicking around, doing fancy tricks on their skateboards and BMXs. Others joined in when they had the chance.

'You sure this is a good idea, Guv?'

'Miss Davies, you remember? Miss Davies said she saw the gang in the vicinity and that lot are some of the E2 according to our gang database. And as for him…'

Aaron performed a trick on his skateboard that went slightly awry, sending the board flying one way, him the other. He just about managed to retain his balance, although he had to do a windmill impersonation to do so.

'What about the cocky bleeder?'

'You'll find out.'

'Look, I know we're following a line of enquiry,' Watts whined. 'It's just … these kids aren't murderers, they're all mouth and no bollocks.'

'Individually, maybe. As a gang, who knows? All these postcode gangs are trying to be the toughest ones on the block and this lot are no exception.' She looked pointedly at him. 'So, you got a better idea?'

'House to house might throw something up.'

'Yeah, right,' Taylor said sarcastically. 'It happened down an alley … and what was he doing down that alley? It wasn't on his route home.'

'Could've stopped for a slash and someone jumped him.'

Taylor grimaced, not having that. 'But why? He still had his wallet on him, so no, not a robbery gone wrong … and Charlie Archer wasn't a man who pissed in alleyways.'

'How about an old score settled? You said he was an old style villain. Maybe someone was still holding a grudge,' Watts ventured. Taylor shook her head, not really having that one either. 'Talking of which, has the brother been traced yet?' he asked.

'Spanish police are on it,' Taylor said, then mumbled, 'and that's a meeting I'm not looking forward to.' She opened her car door. 'Come on, let's rattle some cages.'

'I would never have been able to pull this off. I don't even really know what the internet is and as for booking a flight at such short notice…'

Richie looked into Carmen's eyes as they stood at the foot of the escalator leading up to customs and immigration and the international departure lounge.

'It's part of what I do,' she said. 'Just press buttons.'

'Well, thanks anyway, my darling.'

Carmen's face tightened up as she fought back a tear, but Richie smiled warmly and hugged her tenderly. When they drew apart, she said, 'Please don't do anything silly. I want you back here in one piece.'

'I won't and I will be,' he promised. He picked up his holdall, gave her a nod and stepped onto the moving stairs.

He didn't look back. He was focused now.

Carmen watched the black-clad figure turn left at the top and disappear, petrified she would never see him again.

***

They were smug, arrogant and disrespectful in the way that a lot of disaffected young people were towards the police, but Taylor wasn't intimidated, even as the bikers and the skateboarders whizzed around her and Watts, encircling them. Very few people scared her and she had dealt with hundreds of youths like these every day since the first time she had set foot out in uniform, too long ago to recall now.

Ultimately, she held the power, the one vested in her as a constable – for despite the rank, that was what she still was fundamentally – to take away someone's freedom and as much as people like gang members postured and sneered, not one of them liked losing their liberty and being chucked in a cell. That was always a great leveller.

The two detectives flashed their warrant cards.

Aaron emerged from the circling pack, a look of surprise on his face. 'Well, well, well,' he said, 'you're a fed.' He was looking at Taylor, weighing her up appreciatively.

'Have we met before? No, I don't think so,' Taylor said.

Aaron continued to smirk and eye her. 'You lookin' for me?'

DK was at his shoulder, smouldering with feral sexuality and violence, her eyes all over both Taylor and Watts. 'What you want? Got no crime to solve, so you come hasslin' us law abiding folk?'

Taylor ignored her. To Aaron she said, 'I want a little word with you.'

'What if I say no?'

DK circled Taylor, licking her lips, pouting and pursing her mouth. 'Now I see what the MILF thing is all about,' she said dirtily.

Taylor gave her a withering look, then she focused on Aaron and jerked her head in the direction of her car. He stared back, resolute.

'Trust me, it's just as easy to do this down the nick.' She leaned to him and spoke just loud enough for him to hear. 'But I know how you like to keep your name off the record, Aaron.'

Aaron stared at her and blood drained from his face, but then he got a grip of himself and spun to the gang. 'Make sure you get this on film. You know what the feds are like for fucking up innocent people.'

DK pulled out her phone and began to film, a gesture designed to make Taylor wary. Instead, Taylor leaned to Aaron again and said, 'You might want to tell her not to record sound, know what I mean?'

***

Aaron slouched on the bonnet of Taylor's cars, arms folded defensively. 'This ain't cool, looks well sus,' he moaned.

'I know why you don't have a record,' Taylor waded in straight away.

The lad's face fell. 'I ain't a grass no more. Fuck that. I'm older and wiser now.' His eyes moved from Taylor to Watts and back again, uncomfortable yet defiant yet just a bit vulnerable.

Watts' mouth popped open a touch as he understood what had just been said.

'So we're clear, I do not approve of what happened with my predecessor,' Taylor stated.

'His big promotion? You well jealous, I bet.'

She smirked. 'Getting promoted for overlooking your crimes isn't what I would call good policing, Aaron.'

'But you got a lot bigger fish, so everyone's happy,' he argued his case.

'Apart from your victims,' Watts said.

'That's all behind me now. I was young and stupid.'

Watts cocked an eyebrow and thought, 'You're still that, lad.' Aaron caught the expression and bridled.

'Don't you look at me like that. Ain't a day goes by without me feelin' sick about working for you pricks.'

It was Watts' turn to bridle. 'Talk like that to me again, sunshine, and I'll knock you into next week – and I don't care who the fuck is filming.'

The two males had instantly taken a big dislike to each other and though neither of them realised they were doing it, their spines straightened so each was at his full height and their chests expanded. Primeval stuff.

Taylor almost laughed, although it would have been quite nice to see Aaron visiting the future. She knew Watts was quite capable of seeing to that. Instead she cut through the testosterone with a gentle touch on Watts' forearm. She asked Aaron, 'Where were you at ten o'clock last night?'

'Can't remember, why?'

'Try,' Watts said.

'With DK and the lads, watching a movie.'

'What movie?' Taylor asked.

'Some gangster shit.'

'Where?'

'DK's place.'

'From when to when?' Taylor asked.

He shrugged. 'Eight, maybe, up to midnight.'

'Odd, that,' Taylor said thoughtfully.

'Why?'

'Someone fitting your description was seen in the streets near the Dover Castle pub sometime after 10pm.'

'Nah – I was with the boys an' DK all night.'

'So you were with the gang all night?' she asked.

'Good as.'

'Never by yourself?'

'Nah.'

'Good,' Watts said. 'We were hoping you'd say that because the witness gave a good description of some of your mates, too.'

Aaron was not fazed by the verbal trap. 'Nah, all bull.'

'A man was attacked,' Taylor told him.

'It's a shockin' bad area ... never goes there myself if I can help it,' he grinned.

'He died,' she said, watching him intently for a flicker of something, emotion, guilt perhaps. 'So whoever did it is going down for murder, for life.'

Aaron remained impassive, but Taylor could tell it was a fake barrier. She ploughed on, 'So whoever did this is going down for murder,' she reiterated, 'because that's what it was, a cold blooded killing.'

Still nothing from Aaron.

'Whoever did this won't get a second chance ... there won't be any opportunity to turn grass on this one.'

'Again,' Watts stressed.

Aaron eyeballed them both, waiting for more, seeing they had nothing else. He smiled. 'Well, good luck in catching whoever killed the old guy. If I hear anything be sure to let you know.'

'Like a good citizen,' Watts said, his testosterone still drumming through his system.

'Well thanks for your time, Aaron ... I'll be seeing you,' Taylor promised him.

'Can't wait.' He smiled at her, winked at Watts, then strutted back across the skate park where the others were waiting. The group now included Dean. Aaron joined them like a returning hero, laughing, high-fiving and fist-bumping.

Watts' face was hard. 'Bet we could search them all now and find some weed.'

'Not worth the paperwork. It'd inconvenience us as much as them,' Taylor said practically. She walked to the driver's door wondering if there was any significance in the fact that she had only mentioned that a man had been killed. Aaron had been more specific when he referred to an 'old guy.'

***

They watched the detectives drive away, many pairs of eyes following the progress of the car onto the main road and away.

'What was that?' DK asked.

'The ol' guy, he's dead,' Aaron declared proudly, his head bobbing as he recalled how brilliant it had felt to stamp a man's head out of shape.

Dean had had the feeling the man was dead, but knowing for sure made him want to vomit. The others were more jubilant and when DK said, 'Serve 'im right,' there was a murmur of general agreement.

'But she said someone seen us,' Aaron told them.

'She fishin', or maybe that old bitch grassed,' DK suggested.

'Didn't say nothing about that old lady. She wouldn't talk anyway, she knows better ... I gave her the fingers.' Aaron made the gun shape with his hand.

'We dint see no-one else,' DK said.

Aaron suddenly seemed to have an epiphany. 'But someone else was there ... and we need to do two things ... let's go.'

Aaron set off on his skate board and the rest of E2 followed obediently with the exception of Dean who pretended his shoelaces needed sorting and then, unnoticed by the others, he streaked off in another direction.

SEVEN

Susan Taylor sighed heavily and wondered if she was worrying about nothing.

The fact was she had searched the Metropolitan Police's intelligence and criminal databases, put searches into the Police National Computer and the Criminal Record Office and to be fair to Charlie and Richie Archer, the cupboard was bare – unless you reached right to the back of it.

It was at that point she felt like her fingers had been caught in a bloody big mousetrap.

It was almost 25 years since there had been anything on police records for either of the brothers, something that Taylor actually found odd. The sudden stop, the sudden dead end.

There was more on Wikipaedia than on police files for fuck's sake.

But even on that sometimes useful, often misleading site, there was nothing up to date about the men.

She rubbed her eyes, still gritty after the long night, and began to jot bits down just to keep things in her mind and come to terms with exactly what she was dealing with.

Two brothers born in the East End of London just before the Second World War ended. Charlie the eldest by about fifteen months and the mother, Bernice Archer dying with complications following the birth of her second son, Richie. The two kids were therefore brought up by their father.

His name was Michael – Mickey – Archer, and he had been a villain of the highest order. He had somehow dodged the draft and gone on to make a fortune from the war, as some people did.

He ran a well-organised gang in the East End based on betting, prostitution and the black market, but he was fiercely protective of his two sons. He ensured they had an education and were well brought up and loved. However, their drift into crime as a way of life was inevitable and in their teens they became enforcers for their father around about the 1960 mark, both then in their mid-to-late teens.

Unfortunately they were given the keys to the door in 1963 when there was some very unpleasant underworld fallout following the Great Train Robbery when a Royal Mail train heading between Glasgow and London in the early hours of Thursday 8th August was stopped, attacked and robbed of about £2.5 million.

Mickey Archer had been involved in the periphery of the planning of the heist, which became one of the world's most infamous robberies. He expected to be paid a percentage of the take as promised to him by 'The Silent Man' Charlie Wilson, probably the most dangerous of the robbers, who was also treasurer of the gang.

But Wilson was arrested a couple of weeks after the robbery and sentenced to thirty years for his part before he could share out Mickey's loot.

To Susan Taylor, things then became a little cloudy and there was a lot of speculation as to what happened next and who was involved and not – which was the problem with Wikipaedia. That said, she believed most of what she read.

On a promise that Mickey would receive his share if he broke Wilson out of jail, he and two others sprang him from Winson Green Prison, Birmingham by breaking into the prison and then freeing him.

During an argument that followed – again over the distribution of the money – it was alleged, though never proven, that Wilson shot Mickey Archer dead.

From that moment on, the sons took over the father's business.

Taylor waded through this mass of information, reading about the growth of a criminal empire led by the brothers whose activities covered a multitude of sins from drug trafficking, contract killing, to money laundering and just plain murder – and everything else between.

'Ruthless fucking bastards,' Taylor muttered.

It was unclear to her what happened around the late 1980's when it all seemed to wind up, but she did see there was a terrible gang war all across London during that period when a lot of very dead people were either dredged out of the Thames with much of their faces obliterated and fingers missing, or people simply vanished off the face of the earth. As she sifted through the meagre information that was held on computer, she knew that to find out more she would have to pay a physical visit to Scotland Yard's archives. That didn't fill her with any sense of joy and maybe it wasn't necessary anyway.

She was dealing with the death of an old man who was once a gangster. That was all. Hopefully.

One thing did make her frown, though, was that just after Richie Archer went off the radar, Charlie Wilson, the Great Train Robber, was found shot dead at his villa in Marbella in 1990, a crime for which no one was ever arrested.

Taylor's mouth twitched thoughtfully as she put up one last mug shot and looked at it for a long time: a younger Richie Archer – and what a good looking bastard he was.

She picked up the phone from her desk and dialled an internal number: DC Graham Watts.

'Graham, it's Susan … let's go out and have a walk-through of the crime scene again.'

She had spent too much time staring at a computer screen. It was time to do a bit of Bobbying.

***

The flight was uneventful. Richie had simply sat back in the tight space allocated to him on the budget airline seat, tipped his head and closed his eyes for the two hour journey. On landing he went straight through Customs no problem, then passed through the baggage reclaim area without having to wait for a suitcase because all he had was hand luggage.

As he emerged through the arrival doors, there was a row of people behind a barrier waiting expectantly for loved ones, business associates and the like, some holding up signs with names scribbled on.

Richie scanned the line, then saw the man who was waiting for him.

His name was Roy Edwards and he was similarly dressed to Richie – black suit, black socks, black shoes. His hair was shaved to the scalp and he looked mean and still very fit despite being 69 years old.

They met at the end of the barrier and embraced.

'Good to see you again, Roy.'

'And you, Richie … just sorry the circumstances aren't … well…'

'I know,' Richie said, understanding.

He took Richie's holdall and the two men headed for the exit.

Richie would have been hard-pressed to say that he enjoyed the tedious journey from the airport into central and East London … he felt it was rather like driving into someone's bowels.

***

'So he comes out here,' DI Taylor said on the steps of the Dover Castle. 'Had a drink or two, but not pissed, turns left and starts to walk home along Tent Street.'

Watts nodded, checking his note book as she spoke.

'Doesn't have to walk too far.' She set off at a pace, leaving Watts behind for a moment before he glanced up and realised she'd gone. They walked past the Chicken Hut, which was closed, Taylor pointing at it. 'Anyone visited this place yet? Needs doing.'

'Why?'

'Just does … could have their own security cameras … in fact,' she stopped as suddenly as she'd started. She put her nose right up to the front window and shaded her eyes, peering in. Up behind the counter she saw a camera which faced out across the eating area towards the front of the restaurant, although the word 'restaurant' kind of stuck in Taylor's throat. 'It does … it could have picked up Charlie Archer walking past, maybe.' She looked at Watts. 'Check it.'

'Will do, Guv, when they open up.'

She nodded and strode on, reaching the end of the alley, the entrance to the crime scene, where she stopped again. It was still cordoned off, a young PC standing guard.

'Like I said, Graham, and I'm not being funny, but I know there are some blokes who will piss anywhere, but I'm sure that Charlie Archer wasn't one of them. He would not step out of a pub, then decide he needed a slash like a lot of the scrotes we deal with. He would have gone back into the pub or waited until he got home.'

'I agree.'

'So he got to the alley and went down it for some other reason. Something attracted his attention, or somebody called out and ambushed him … but the attack was so ferocious and the motive obviously wasn't robbery … I don't think he was the … er, fuck, what do I think?' she stopped herself and rearranged her thoughts. 'He saw something he shouldn't have done, went for a look and his curiosity, or whatever, got him killed – and that's my hypothesis.'

'I agree.'

'You agree a lot.'

'I'm a very agreeable person.'

'Matter of opinion,' Taylor said. 'What I want to do is get my ducks in a row, then pull in that E2 gang one at a time, the weakest first, and start twisting the bastards.'

'I agree.'

***

They did a mass strip at JP's place. Every member, including DK who didn't even hesitate to take off her clothes, who had been at the scene of the murder was ordered by Aaron to remove all their gear that they'd been wearing the night before - and most were still in exactly the same stuff – including footwear, and put it all into the plastic bin bags he had provided.

'Why? Why the fuck?' one of them protested. He had taken off his trainers and was inspecting the soles. 'I luv these.'

Aaron snatched them off him and threw them into the bag.

'Ain't got no blood on 'em,' the lad whined.

'Forensics, dimwit,' Aaron glared at him. 'Just cos you can't see it, don' mean it ain't there, init? We got to clean ourselves up good and proper cos if they comes looking for us, they'll strip us and swab us and our kit.'

When they had finished and changed into fresh gear, Aaron gave the plastic bags to JP who knew someone who worked in a local factory that had a furnace into which it was all going to go.

Aaron looked at everybody. 'That everybody?'

It was, with one exception.

'Dean,' he said quietly.

***

Roy pulled his old Singer Gazelle into the side of the road just past the Dover Castle. Richie paused for a few moments, inhaling the surroundings which he knew well and had been part of his and Charlie's manor in the old days. His face was tight as he controlled his emotions. Then he climbed out of the car and walked towards the taped-off alleyway, Richie taking in everything.

'What a shit hole. He deserved better than this,' he commented.

'Oi, I still live here, you know,' Roy protested. He was right behind Richie.

The two old comrades shared a knowing glance and approached the alley and the young PC standing guarding the entrance. He saw that the two men were en route to head down the alley and moved across to block their path, holding up his hands.

'Sorry gents, this is closed…'

'Because of the tape?' Roy asked as Richie sidestepped the constable and went straight through the tape, snapping it as if he was going through the winning post. The cop was open-mouthed and went to stop him, but Roy stepped into his path.

'Leave him … and have more conviction in what you say next time, son. I didn't believe you,' Roy said to the PC, then turned and followed Richie into the alley.

***

The two detectives were at the wheelie bin in discussion about the crime scene. They glanced up and saw the two men striding towards them.

Watts broke away from Taylor and went to them. 'Sorry, sirs, this is a closed crime scene.'

Richie halted, eyed Watts from head to toe and back again, then said, 'Out of my way, son, I want to talk to the organ grinder.'

Watts misunderstood the word 'organ'. 'Huh?' By which time Richie had circumvented him and been replaced by a chuckling Roy, who said, 'Not that kind of organ, son.'

Richie was face to face with Taylor.

Something shimmered through her body at the sight of Richie Archer who, it had to be said, had got here much quicker than she had thought possible. She realised then what that 'something' was. It was a heady mix of excitement and trepidation on at last coming nose-to-nose with probably the most dangerous villain she had ever met in her career. And it did not matter that he was knocking on the door of 70 years old because there was still something smouldering about him, something untamed and feral. It was in the eyes. It was always in the eyes.

Even so, she refused to be intimidated by him.

'This where it happened then?' Richie demanded. He pointed to the dried blood stains on the ground.

'Richie Archer,' she began.

He glanced at her appreciatively. 'Good – at least you've got some detective skills.' Then he looked pityingly at Watts who, even in such a short space of time, had not impressed him at all.

'I have the ability to use a computer,' she said.

'Oh, that's nice. I don't,' he said. 'As I say, at least you're doing something to find out who killed my brother.'

She moved closer to him. 'I'm Detective Inspector Taylor. I'm in charge of this investigation. I'm very sorry about your brother,' she said, trying to establish some control.

'I know you are and I'm sure you are … but what can you tell me?'

Taylor knew she had to retain that control, otherwise this man would trample all over her. 'Can we move to one side? This, as my colleague explained, is still a crime scene and I do not wish to contaminate it.' She stressed the word contaminate.

Richie hesitated, then complied and stepped to the side of the alley with her.

'Like I said, what can you tell me?'

'Not much, I'm afraid … we still don't know how or why he ended up in the alley, let alone…'

'Who killed him?' Richie finished her sentence for her.

'Well, I…' she stammered. 'It's very early in the investigation.'

He eyeballed her and she felt his power. She almost flinched, but then straightened up.

Richie saw this in her and smiled, liking her strength. He could feel she was a good cop, though maybe not one who could move as quickly for him as he would have wanted.

'Nice to have met you, Inspector.' He gave her a mock salute and spun to leave. He had seen enough.

'Mr Archer,' she called him back. 'There are certain formalities I need to go through with you, I'm afraid.'

***

She had been looking at herself in the mirror for a very long time, standing there almost in a trance, trying to work out exactly who she was, what she had become and what she wanted to be … what she felt.

She wasn't certain, except in answer to the last part.

She felt incredibly sad and maybe dirty, defiled and violated.

She jumped with a start when the doorbell rang, followed by the sound of a fist hammering on the door. Her sad face turned into a scared one. She edged towards the window and peeped out through a crack in the closed curtains.

From the front door, an out of breath Dean Walker looked up pleadingly.

She drew back quickly, afraid.

Dean hammered again, then began pacing nervously, his eyes scanning in all directions, head shaking, muttering to himself, 'Come on, come on…'

She took the decision and opened her bedroom window.

'Lauren, are you okay?' Dean panted.

Her contempt for him was almost physical. 'Fuck you! You were going to rape me.'

'No … no … no way.' His voice was desperate. 'I didn't know Aaron was going to do that. I didn't even realise you and Aaron were…' Now his voice trailed off to nothing and a look of shame came to his face.

'It was a big mistake, okay?' she said.

'I was gonna rescue you,' Dean said.

'As if…'

'Yeah, I was, and then that old guy came along and then it all went to rat shit … and even if it was a mistake, you and Aaron … he's coming here right now cos he thinks you're going to tell the police.'

'Tell them what? That he tried to rape me? Maybe I fucking will.'

'If you do that, Lauren, he'll kill you … like … like he killed the old man.'

The words hit Lauren like a thunderbolt. She was aghast. 'He's dead?'

'He's well dead,' Dean confirmed, a crick in his neck as he looked up at her. 'Please, Lauren, I don't want you to get hurt. I,' he began, then his head twisted one way, then the other and he uttered, 'Oh fuck, he's coming … I need to hide.'

Dean sprinted down the side of Lauren's house, vaulted the dividing fence and ducked behind next door's shed.

Lauren slammed and locked the window then hurtled down stairs, running to the front door, slotting the upper and lower bolts in place. Then she ran back through to the kitchen at the rear of the house, ensuring the back door was also fully secure. She extracted the largest carving knife from the wooden block, then sank to her knees by the kitchen cupboards.

Ian Ogilvy as Richie Archer

Alison Doody as Susan Taylor

Roy (Chris Ellison) and Butch (Tony Denham)
in action

Arthur (James Cosmo) brings out the heavy
artillery

Aaron (Danny-Boy Hatchard) is the terrifying
new breed of gangster

The E2 Gang swarm all over the hospital

The Archer Gang extracting information…
The Old Way!

DK (Red Madrell) attempts to kill Richie

Lysette Anthony as Lizzie Davis

The E2 Gang pay a hospital visit

Richie Archer (Ian Ogilvy)
with one of his closest friends

Richie lays down the law, old style!

Lauren (Dani Dyer) is taken captive
by Aaron (Danny-Boy Hatchard)

Richie (Ian Ogilvy) discusses the merits of old
style diplomacy with Houghton (Nicky Henson)

Richie (Ian Ogilvy) about to dispense
some old style medicine

The doorbell rang.

Lauren's heart began slamming hard against her rib cage. Pounding with terror. A horrible taste gushed into her mouth.

In her hand, the knife trembled.

She took a very quick glimpse down the hallway, saw shapes moving on the other side of the frosted glass of the front door.

The doorbell rang again. The letterbox clattered.

Lauren whipped her head back, gripped the knife with both hands.

She was petrified.

Then the doorbell stopped, but only for a moment, as the hammering and baying began instead.

Fists on the front door, against the living room windows, then the kitchen door as the gang split and came around the back. Lauren scrambled into a corner, wanting to disappear, hugging herself.

Bang, bang, bang. It was a siege.

And then the battering stopped as suddenly as it had begun.

Lauren raised her head slowly, not daring to draw breath, trying to stifle the sobs that threatened to make her whole body explode.

'Lauren … Lauren,' Aaron's voice cooed. 'I know you're in there … I can smell the pig shit … I know you're listening.'

She crawled across to the kitchen door and peeped down the hallway again, could see the letterbox tilted open and the obscene shape of Aaron's mouth moving as he spoke through the gap.

'About the other night … my boys were a bit disappointed not to get what I promised. I'd built it up, see. Telling them how good you were at being a sket.'

Lauren tried desperately hard to keep quiet and still, but Aaron's voice chilled her to the bone marrow, terrified her.

'Now, my boys do as I say,' Aaron continued, 'so if you keep quiet about things, I won't let them near you, but if you mention anything about me to anyone' – he shouted that last word – 'thing is, you see, I know who your mum is and I will let my dogs loose on you both.'

The letterbox clattered shut, making Lauren jump, and the doorbell began to ring.

***

'Is this the body of your brother, Charlie Archer?'

They were standing in the mutedly-lit viewing room of the public mortuary, a room divided in half by a wall down the centre and a large window.

Members of the public were led into one side.

The body to be identified was wheeled in on a trolley to the other side of the window and when everything was prepared, the purple curtain was drawn back by a mortuary attendant, who then pulled off the muslin sheet covering the actual face of the body.

Taylor glanced at Richie.

He stood resolute and emotionless as the curtain was pulled back and the vampire-faced mortuary attendant slowly revealed the body underneath the shroud.

Charlie's severely crushed face looked even more dreadful. It was twisted out of shape, the jaw jutting out at an abnormal angle, his mouth sagging open, his teeth visible. His head was ballooned and swollen and his eyes were a dirty black colour, one of them open, the other shut, and his nose was crushed flat.

Taylor thought she heard something escape from Richie's throat, but when she looked, he did not appear to have to reacted to the disturbing sight other than with a flare of his nostrils. However, although his eyes seemed dead, Taylor could sense the fire of rage building inside him.

'Mr Archer. Is this your brother, Charlie?'

'I heard you the first time.'

'Sorry.'

Richie nodded. 'Yes, it is my brother.'

'Thank you.' Taylor looked through the window at the attendant who re-covered the body, then drew the curtain. 'I'm so very sorry,' she said genuinely. 'Unfortunately, this,' – she indicted the location, the process – 'is one of those things we can't avoid doing, but now that we have done, we can arrange a post mortem which will probably take place later today.'

'For why?' Richie asked.

'To tell us how he died.'

'I can tell you right now how he died.' Richie's eyes settled on her face. She swallowed. 'I don't need a fucking post mortem for that.' He turned to leave.

Roy Edwards and DC Watts were waiting at the back of the room.

Sensing something, Taylor quickly said, 'Mr Archer.' He stopped, but did not turn. 'I know your reputation and I know there are inevitably certain divisions between us, but let me be clear … if you interfere with my investigation in any way, I'll put you inside.'

'Is that it?'

'Yes.'

He turned, gave her an enigmatic smile that would have befitted the devil himself, then jerked his head at Roy and they left the viewing room together, slamming the door behind them.

A nervy Watts sidled up to Taylor. 'You know that old saying?' he asked her.

'What old saying would that be?'

'I wouldn't want to meet him in a dark alley. I get what all the fuss is about now,' Watts admitted.

EIGHT

Even though she was looking at her iPad, pretending to read the novel she had electronically downloaded, her mind wasn't on it and the words were just a blur.

Lizzy swiped the screen all the way back to the beginning of the book because, actually, none of it had gone in which frustrated her because she liked nothing better than to settle back and read Martina Cole's latest female gangster thriller.

She sighed, her mind in turmoil, wondering if somehow her life had now changed for the worse. Even though she wasn't directly involved in the murder, she knew that anyone touched by a crime of this magnitude was always changed in some way.

And then there was Richie Archer.

To phone him had taken a lot of courage, but she had done and had heard his voice again. It was older, gruffer, but definitely Richie Archer, and hearing it had sent shiver down her spine.

The fact that he also remembered her thrilled her, even if he did say he remembered everyone. Even if she was just one of many, when he had gone on to describe her, the feeling deep inside was something she had not experienced for a long, long, long time.

To put it bluntly, he had made her moist.

She thought about that and squirmed a little on the couch, a dirty little grin on her lips as she vividly imagined something that had never happened, never would happen, happening in her mind's eye. She was in a gooey, dreamy world all of her own when it was interrupted by the sound of her doorbell – not the only thing that was ringing at that moment.

Crossly she shelved all thoughts of Richie Archer doing very naughty things to her, got up and went to the window to look out.

Her face fell in shock when she saw who was standing there. She pulled back quickly, her breath suddenly short.

The bell rang again.

It took a few moments to pull herself together, smooth down her skirt, check herself in the mirror, tucking back a few wisps of stray hair, then, sliding back the door bolts, opening up to her visitor.

'Hello Lizzy,' Richie Archer said, smiling that smile.

***

He sat on the armchair, cup of tea in hand, legs crossed, watching Lizzy speak as she sat across from him on the sofa. He tried not to think about how things could have been between them. His focus was in the here and now.

'This E2 lot, we're nothing to them,' she was telling him, trying to overcome her self-consciousness as his eyes concentrated on her. 'They got no respect for us, no one to stand up to them, see? Even the coppers are bloody clueless or scared.'

He sipped his tea, which tasted wonderful. No matter how hard he tried, it was impossible to truly replicate a good British brew out in Spain. The water from the reservoirs that supplied London was just far superior to anything over there, and that was the key – the water.

'Yes, I got that impression.'

'It's all different from…' she started to say.

'From my day?' he ventured.

Lizzy shrugged. 'At least we could walk the streets back then. You didn't allow stuff like this to happen.'

'Innocents?' Richie suggested.

She nodded. 'I'm just glad my old man…' She paused and sniffed back memories. She may not have ended up with Richie but she did have a good marriage to another man who had cared for her and who had died too soon.

Richie placed his cup down on the coffee table and stood up.

'Thanks for the tea, and your help.'

'I just wish I could tell you more. Charlie was a nice fella in spite of … y'know,' she faltered.

'His past?' Richie smiled. 'I know … listen, it might be better if the police don't know I've been here, okay? It might … complicate things.'

Lizzy stood and led Richie to the front door where, with her fingers on the lock, she turned and leaned against the wall. 'I never thought in all my days that you'd be in my house … I just wish you were forty years younger.'

Richie grinned cheekily and gave her an amused, salacious once-over that made her blush bright red.

'Not that!' she said unconvincingly. 'I meant I'd feel safer if you were still around … everyone would … in those days we knew what was what, where you could go, where you couldn't … these days, it's different. Ain't no safe paths through the jungle any more.'

They held each other's eyes, then Lizzy opened the door and Richie slid out past her, brushing against her as she wanted him to do.

She closed the door behind him.

Outside Richie stood and listened to the security chain being put back on, the bolts being slid across, the key turning in the lock. He glanced over his shoulder and saw Lizzy's outline through the frosted glass, sighed thoughtfully.

It just wasn't the same as it used to be.

***

Dean perched on the end of Lauren's bed, leaning forwards, elbows on his thighs, his fingers interlaced.

He looked humble.

Lauren was edgy, though. She wasn't sure this was a good move, allowing Dean into the house. After all, he was one of them. He had always been there since she had met Aaron, but when she forced herself to remember, Dean had always been on the edge of everything, hesitant to get involved as if his heart wasn't fully into it, as if he was searching for some meaning or to be part of something, and realising that being in E2 wasn't the answer.

'I'm so sorry for not stopping what happened,' Dean admitted. He was staring at the floor.

Lauren softened as, still rewinding her memory, she now saw Dean taking sneaky, appreciative looks at her, then looking quickly away before she spotted him. Even then, under Aaron's influence, she liked the look of Dean.

'It's not like you could have stopped them all.'

'You say that, but an old man did.' He raised his face and looked at her meaningfully. His lips quivered as he thought about his own cowardice. 'An old guy stepped up to the mark and took them on. I didn't. What does that say about me?'

Lauren had been sitting at the top of the bed, keeping her distance, her legs folded underneath her. She slid up into a proper sitting position and moved along the bed to sit next to him. She placed an arm around his shoulders.

'Why are you with E2?' she asked.

He blinked back tears. 'Part of something … excitement, fun, y'know … a bit bad, maybe.'

'What does your mum think?'

He shook his head, not wanting to go there. 'What about yours?'

'She'd be off the scale. She doesn't know.'

There was silence. Lauren's arm was draped across his shoulders. He angled his head sideways and their faces were only inches apart.

Lauren's lips parted softly. She moved her hand up onto the back of Dean's shaved head and gently pulled him towards her. Their lips met tenderly.

***

Even on its third viewing, the impact of the attack was not lessened. It was brutal, sustained and horrifying to watch.

The images were in focus, then blurred, then back in focus, the hand held camera moving jerkily, trying to keep up with the assault, the kicking, the beating, and that point where Charlie Archer, after having been savaged by a vicious mob, had still risen and spoken.

Some on the words were inaudible, but not the last two: 'You coward.' And then he spat out blood and possibly a broken tooth.

Then the foot lashed out and that voice was clear. 'One-on-one? You got it, mate.'

Then the stomping of Charlie's head began, then the screen went blank. It was over.

Richie and Roy stared at the screen of the iPad, flanked by Lizzy and Giles, the landlord of the Dover Castle.

They were standing in a huddle at the open end of the bar with Giles having to leave occasionally to see to other customers.

Richie stood upright.

'You got to be proud of him, Rich,' Roy said. 'He still had it right up to the last and if there hadn't been so many of them…'

Richie moved away, his face as hard as granite. He stalked across the floor of the pub, a terrible anger gripping his heart.

He stopped at Lizzy and in disbelief said, 'And people – kids – put stuff like this online, or whatever you call it?' He grasp of the internet was tenuous.

She nodded. 'My grandson found it this morning. It's on what known as the dark net.'

'The dark net? What the hell's that?' Richie said. He and Roy stared uncomprehendingly at Lizzy. Richie glanced at Giles for help, but all he got was a shrug.

'Well I'm no expert,' Lizzy said. 'I just muddle my way through things as best I can, because I have to, but the kids are whizzo with it.'

'And the dark net?' Richie insisted.

'It's a private network and only trusted people can access it,' she explained.

'Right … and your grandson?'

'Spends eight hours a day on his computer. He's accessed the dark net before, but he says it's tricky and no-one else ever knows he's been there.'

Richie grimaced, looked at Giles again, who said, 'I have no idea what she just said.'

Lizzy scanned the confused faces and said, 'Let me put this in terms you old blokes might understand. Picture this,' she said, drawing an imaginary square with her forefingers. 'This is a window and the curtains are drawn, yeah?' They still looked mystified – but intrigued. 'And in the room beyond is a couple … er, making love.' She couldn't help but eye Richie for a fleeting moment. 'But there's a tiny crack in the curtain.'

'Christ, I wondered what you were going to say then,' Roy guffawed. 'A tiny crack…'

She gave him a withering look. Richie shook his head sadly. Giles snickered like a pre-pubescent teen.

'And someone looks through the crack and sees what's going on … humping … but he's not supposed to be there.'

'A peeping Tom,' Richie said.

'Correct … and more often than not, the peeping Tom will get away, but if he falls off the upturned bin he's standing on, all hell breaks loose and the world and his dog are after him. The secret of looking into these dark nets is not to get caught, and my grandson is so good, he always gets away.'

Richie snapped the mood and went back to the issue in hand. 'Does your grandson know any of these lads?'

Lizzy shook her head. 'But they look like the lot I saw. I swear it. I can print off some screen grabs.'

'What?' Richie's face screwed up. Clearly the technological world had left him behind.

'I can zoom in on their faces,' Lizzy explained patiently, 'and print photos, mug shots. They might not be totally clear but we can show them to the police. It might help.'

'No,' Richie said firmly. 'We keep this to ourselves, right?' His eyes moved from one to the other, making his point.

'But why? This could help them,' Lizzy said.

Richie leaned on the bar next to her, shoulder to shoulder. She could feel his power radiating. 'Help them what, Lizzy? Get justice? And what kind of justice would that be? A slap on the wrists? A few months in a glorified hotel?'

'It's the law, Richie,' she said, so aware of how close their faces were to each other. 'It's all we've got.'

'Not for me … someone crosses me I prefer to deal with it myself. Let me have those screen thingies … their faces … do that for me.' He touched her forearm and she remembered the old Richie and nodded agreement.

'Here, look at this,' Giles interrupted. He had been messing with Lizzy's iPad. He was staring intently at the screen, but then slid the device across the bar and swivelled it around so Richie, Roy and Lizzy could see. 'I looked at some of the other stuff on the dark net and saw this.' He pressed play.

Lizzy put her hand to her mouth as she watched a young girl being dragged and held over a wheelie bin, her skirt jerked up, exposing her bottom. She struggled in vain against the multitude of hands that gripped her and at one point whoever was shooting the scene focused in closely on the girl's face.

'Oh, poor girl.' Lizzy said. Then her eyes narrowed. 'I recognise her, I think.'

Then, just a moment before the screen went blank and filming stopped, there was a man's loud voice out of shot.

'Oi – what's going on?'

The image went and that same cold rage that had squeezed Richie's heart only moments before surged back again. 'That's Charlie's voice,' he said.

'And that's the place where he was killed,' Roy added. 'That alleyway,' he jerked his thumb, 'just up from here.'

'I remember the bin,' Richie said.

Giles tapped and swiped the screen on the iPad and rewound the clip, then set it going again. When it came to the girl's face, he paused it.

'Yeah,' Lizzy confirmed, 'I do know her … she's local. I know where she works.'

'And now it all slots into place,' Richie said. 'Now we know what Charlie was doing in that alleyway.'

***

'You've done good for yourself,' Richie said, admiring the view up the Thames from the penthouse apartment on the river front at Limehouse. It wasn't a new apartment block, but it had been modernised regularly and the two bedroomed apartment where Richie propped himself against the ornate balcony railings was probably valued somewhere in excess of a million. Roy had bought it for cash way back.

Roy joined him, also looking at the view. As the crow flew, they could see the top rim of the London Eye dead ahead of them.

'No, not true,' Roy corrected Richie. 'We all did good for ourselves. It was a joint effort and you know it – and we all got away from it just in time.'

'Took our ill-gotten gains and ran?'

'In a manner of speaking.' Roy raised his glass of Talisker whisky and the two men clinked glasses.

'Good of you to put me up,' Richie said. 'Short notice and all that. I won't be an imposition.'

'You can stay as long as you want, you know that, and I mean it. Good to have a bit of company … lonely since…'

'I know,' Richie said. 'It might get very iffy all this, though.'

'Let it,' Roy shrugged.

They became silent, maudlin even. Then Richie said, 'Funny, innit, you up here lordin' it over everybody – and I don't mean that nasty, like – but Charlie stayed at ground level despite what money he had – and he had a ton of it.'

'Man of the people. Down there was his home, not up here. Just that kinda bloke. Grounded.'

'Mm, yeah,' Richie agreed, thinking, 'and that's what got him killed.'

'Richie?' Roy said cautiously, 'hope you don't mind me asking … I've always wondered…'

Richie held up a warning finger. 'Wherever this is going, first let me ask you, are you wearing a wire and are you a police informant?'

'I'm a supergrass,' Roy confirmed.

'That's okay then … ask away,' Richie laughed.

'Charlie Wilson … the 'silent man'..?'

'Who died 23rd April 1990?'

'Yeah, that Charlie Wilson, the Great Train Robber.'

'What you askin'?' Richie said.

'Was it you? He killed your dad an' everything.'

Richie grinned, made the shape of a gun with his right hand and pointed it at Roy's head. Then he roared with laughter, downed the last drop of his fine whisky and said, 'Bed for me.'

He patted Roy on the shoulder and went inside, leaving him alone on the balcony.

'Well, I'll be fucked, it is true,' Roy said and held up his glass in a toast to his old friend.

NINE

Richie liked the way she looked, but there was something disconcertingly familiar about her which he could not quite pin down.

He had been sitting in a Starbucks café situated diagonally opposite the clothes shop just off Brick Lane in Whitechapel and had seen her go into work and immediately start to revamp the window display of what was a quirky but good quality shop.

Richie sipped the filter coffee of the day. The menu displayed behind the counter had flummoxed him slightly … too many choices and all a bit too fancy for his tastes, so he'd opted for the filter coffee which came with a plus - a free refill.

He sat by the window and watched the world hustle by and realised he had never been in a Starbucks in his life before. He wasn't even sure they had existed when he left the country but he knew one thing for certain, he wasn't in a particular rush to visit one again. They seemed designed to suck you in and spit you out and he thought it was a soulless establishment.

He was astounded by the pace of change. He had been back a couple of times – flying visits for specific purposes and all very discreet and under the radar, which meant under an assumed identity – but those had been in-and-outs, arrive, do business, depart. There hadn't been time to dawdle, particularly when on one visit he had fed a body into a wood chipper and another time watched some other poor unfortunate be crushed in the boot of a car in a scrapyard. No time to look in on old mates, chew the fat. He'd had to move quickly, leave no trail just in case the authorities came for him. To all intents and purposes, he had not even been out of Spain.

He gave the girl in the clothes shop time to settle, get her first job of the day done.

Even Richie could tell she had a good eye and managed to bring alive the window display with colour and depth.

And, yes, she was strangely familiar.

He finished his coffee, placed the mug down in front of him and turned it around full circle, three times, then stood up. He went back to the counter and spoke to the barista.

'I'll be back for my free mug.'

'I'm sorry sir, it doesn't work like that.'

'How does it work?'

'It has to be claimed in the same visit.'

'Doesn't say that on your board.'

'I'm afraid that's how it is,' the young man said patronisingly. Richie simply eyed him malevolently and he seemed to wilt under the gaze. 'But in your case, I'll make an exception.'

'I thought you would. Back in ten minutes.'

He crossed the busy road carefully - even an old gangster wasn't immune to being flattened by a London bus – and entered the clothes shop which was called Aphrodite's Palace. Somewhere at the back of his mind he thought he had once owned a night club of the same name, but wasn't certain.

It was rather like stepping into Dr Who's Tardis in that the small frontage belied that the shop behind was immense. There were rows upon rows of women's clothing on racks and it was very much like a maze. The girl had finished doing the window display and was moving through the rows, tidying and adjusting and rearranging the stock as she did.

Richie weaved his way to her and she smiled professionally and also genuinely at him.

'Hiya, can I help you?'

Richie saw she was wearing a name badge: Lauren.

'I think you can. I need some information.'

'About what?' she smiled knowingly. 'A special present? We have everything here.'

'So I see, but it's not about that.'

'What then?' She was still open, not the least suspicious, but when Richie spoke his next words, they chilled her and her face crumbled.

'The alley off Tent Street.'

'I don't understand,' she said quietly, fear in her voice.

Richie stared at her intensely, waiting. When nothing came, he said, 'I think you do.'

'I'm sorry, but I think you've made a mistake,' Lauren said and backed away as though she was reversing away from a lion about to charge. She started to weave between the rails, Richie with her step by step.

'Don't play games with me, sweetheart.'

Lauren then panicked. She turned and fled into the clothing maze, pulling down a rack behind her as she ran, trying to block Richie's way. He simply stepped across the mess of garments as she ducked sideways and brought another rack crashing down.

He stayed with her, relentless, almost robotic, totally concentrating on following her until she was trapped at a fire exit door at the back of the shop which she turned to and tried to force down the release bar, rattling it ineffectively.

Richie stepped up behind her, reached over and placed his hand on the bar. Lauren spun to face him, recoiling.

Another member of staff ran up, concerned.

'Is everything okay, Lauren?'

Lauren stared at Richie who turned to the other girl. 'We're fine,' he said, then looked at Lauren.' Aren't we, Lauren?'

He pushed down on the release bar and the door swung open outwards.

***

The alleyway stank. As well as backing onto the clothes shop, there were also a number of takeaways on the same stretch with their resultant garbage. Richie saw a big fat rat scamper away … never less than ten feet away from a rat, he thought cynically.

Lauren leaned against the wall, shaking.

'Who are you? You're not a policeman.'

Richie smiled at the thought. 'No, but I do want some answers.'

She raised her face, looked him in the eye. 'I don't know what you mean.'

'My brother died protecting you.'

The words sank in. Then it all walloped her. 'Oh God ... there was nothing I could do,' She tried to hold back her tears, but her face was collapsing in grief.

'I know,' Richie said softly.

'How? How do you know?'

'You're an internet sensation,' he said.

'Oh God,' she uttered again and sank slowly to her haunches, putting her head in her hands. 'They filmed it, didn't they?' The memory was raw.

'Look, I don't care why you've not said anything to anyone. I get it ... but now things have changed.'

'Why?'

'Because I'm here. I just want some names, that's all. Do you know any of them?'

'No ... I ... no,' she said, 'I don't.'

'What they could have done to you,' Richie began, but didn't need to finish because of the expression on her face as she looked up at his through her hands. 'I can see you know who they are.'

'I don't know any of them. I was just attacked,' she insisted implausibly.

'I wish I believed you ... but I don't,' he said. She was still sitting on her heels. 'I don't want to have to resort to anything other than questions to get the information I want, my love, but I will if I have to.'

His penetrating stare and the threat made her quake all the more.

'If they ever found out that I'd...'

Richie's patience had now expired. 'Names,' he demanded.

'I was there with Aaron, who I thought was my boyfriend.'

'Surname? What's his surname? And where does he live?'

'I don't know,' she said, ashamed.

Very little could ever shock Richie Archer. He could understand not knowing the personal details of a one night stand – hell, he'd had enough of them in his time and never known a first name, let alone a last – but when someone said they had a girlfriend or boyfriend, the least he expected was that they knew their last name and address.

'You don't know your boyfriend's surname? What the fuck has happened to this place?'

Lauren could see that, too. It made her feel shit and like a used commodity. 'I was trying to fit in,' she attempted to explain the inexplicable. 'I thought he really liked me...'

'But..?'

'He just used me.'

'How involved was he?' Richie snapped. He had been shocked, she felt bad ... time to move on. No time for deep reflection on society and relationships. Leave that to sociologists and agony aunts.

'He's the ringleader,' Lauren blurted. 'Nothing happens without him saying so.'

'So the buck stops with him? Anyone else?'

Lauren hesitated and looked up at the man standing over her. He was old – decrepit in her eyes – but he had an aura about him that scared her more than Aaron. For an instant she considered fingering Dean, but the kiss on the bed stopped that revelation. Instead she offered up someone else.

'Yeah, I think his name is Maz. He went to my school.'

Richie smiled, part thanks, part anticipation. Things were going to move.

'You're not going to..?' she started to ask.

'Not a word to anyone,' he said, holding up a finger. 'You better get back to work.' He gave her a curt nod then set off down the alley towards the main road.

'Mister?' Lauren called after him. Richie stopped, turned, didn't say anything. 'Be careful, there's so many of them.'

'I was brought up to believe it's about quality, not quantity.'

'He was a good man, your brother. He saved me.'

Richie nodded. 'Then don't let his death be in vain, Lauren. Do something with your life. Forget about those little runts and find someone that deserves you. Life's too short to waste time.' Then he spun on his heels, strode away.

Lauren watched him go, then rose and went back into the shop through the fire exit door.

The alleyway returned to silence and emptiness until a figure emerged from a dark, recessed doorway further down. DK stood there, having heard most of the exchange between

Lauren and the old man. And the big fat rat scampered across the alleyway.

***

Richie hadn't wanted to make a big show of it.

After the post mortem on Charlie had been conducted and it was unarguably obvious what the cause of death had been – massive brain trauma caused by a sustained assault – the coroner had made contact with Richie in order to release the body to him. Sometimes this process could take a long time, but in this case the wheels of justice were oiled by the fact that the coroner for the area was formerly a solicitor on Richie's payroll and he was only too happy to release the body, particularly when £400 fell into his lap.

Richie had then quickly arranged a funeral to take place, again using his old network. This time it was an undertaker who, many years before had provided certain services for Richie, including body disposal and the importation and exportation of drugs in cadavers. Richie had made his requirements clear: no mess, no fuss.

He did not want to bring any undue attention to himself by having a big, brash funeral with something ridiculous on the coffin like a floral display depicting a Tommy Gun. He wanted quiet, discreet and dignified because he was pretty sure that is what Charlie would have also wanted.

What even Richie could not have bargained for was the response of the people.

The small funeral cortege had assembled at Heron's undertakers, in Bethnal Green – now actually run on a day to day basis by old man Heron's granddaughter, a stunning looking, red-haired beauty in her early thirties, who made Richie even think he would not have minded her laying him out in his coffin.

'Just as you ordered, Mr Archer,' she said.

'Thank you, Kathy. May I ask how your grandfather is?'

'Very old, very doddering, but still with all his faculties. He insisted on looking after your brother personally and, of course, waiving all costs.'

'No. That's very kind, but I insist on paying,' Richie said, even though he had put many thousands into George Heron's deep, undertaker pockets over the years.

'As you wish,' she said graciously. 'Would you care to see your brother?'

'Please.'

She smiled and touched his elbow, then led him through to an anteroom at the back of the premises which opened out onto the car park at the rear where the hearse could be accessed.

Charlie Archer was laid out in a casket, dressed in a black tuxedo with a red bow tie, his arms crossed in a saintly way over his chest. By his shoulder was a photograph of his mother and father in a gold frame.

Old man Heron had done a great job of rearranging and touching up Charlie's face, almost breathing life back into him.

'Could I have a moment?' Richie asked Kathy.

He stood by the casket, which was resting on a gurney, and gripped the edge of it. He himself was dressed in a Moss Bros suit he'd hired that morning, which wasn't the best of fits, but was okay.

Richie looked at Charlie's peaceful, resting place.

'It was no way to go,' Richie said. 'Not for a man like you. No dignity, no chance.' But then Richie raised his eyes. 'But maybe I'm wrong there ... maybe this is how you should have gone, dying to protect a vulnerable girl who'd got herself in the shit, and taking on the bastards responsible ... maybe that is exactly how you should have gone, Charlie ... love you, brother.'

He wiped his eyes, turned and walked back into the main waiting area where Kathy Heron was ready to roll.

Two black clad undertakers walked into the anteroom and closed the door.

'We'll get him into the hearse and be on our way,' Kathy Heron said.

When Charlie had been placed in the hearse, Kathy led Richie outside where the two-vehicle only procession was ready to move off. The rear yard of the undertaker's was protected from any curious onlookers by a high brick wall.

Richie had specified a wreath of red roses to be laid on the coffin and that the coffin itself be rested on a bed of ferns – and that was it. He had also unearthed Charlie's never used Rolls Royce from a lock-up garage in Mile End and it was in this, driven by Roy, that Richie would follow Charlie's body to the crematorium in Highbury.

It was a four mile journey.

As Richie climbed in alongside Roy, his friend whispered, 'You might need to brace yourself for this, old friend.'

Richie did not understand what he meant until the gates opened, the hearse set off, the Rolls followed and it was at this point that Richie's breath was taken away and tears formed in his eyes.

As they turned out of the yard onto a side street, Richie got the first inkling. A crowd of onlookers had gathered.

'What the fuck?' he said.

'Hold on to your hat,' Roy said.

The hearse moved from the side street onto the main road at the requisite snail's pace. People also lined that road, hundreds of them. Some, mainly older ones, stepped out as the hearse passed and placed a hand on the side window, their lips moving in silent prayer.

Richie was stunned.

Even though Roy had an idea this was going to happen, he too was virtually speechless. He said, 'These are his people, Richie.'

Richie swallowed something that felt very much like a chunk of coal.

If he expected it to finish at the next junction, he was wrong. People thronged the route, including the slight detour – ordered previously by Richie – which took them past the alleyway where Charlie had been murdered and the Dover Castle.

The pavement at the head of the alley was covered by hundreds of wreaths and bouquets of flowers, stacked high. The 'police do not cross' tapes stretched across the alley entrance provided an ironic backdrop to the flowers.

Richie swallowed again and another tear fell as they drove past the Dover Castle where more than a hundred regulars, including Lizzy and Giles, the landlord, had spilled out from the doors, each one with a glass of wine in hand, raised to Charlie. A banner stretched across the pub wall read, 'Charlie Archer: RIP'.

'I didn't ask for any of this,' Richie said.

'You didn't need to,' Roy told him. 'This is just what we were talking about. He was a man of the people, Richie. This is genuine.'

'They won't do this for me.'

'Nah,' Roy said. 'You'll be feeding fishes in the Med, probably.'

'Bastard,' Richie hissed good naturedly.

It was the same for the whole of the journey, streets lined, people nodding their respects, until the cortege finally arrived at the entrance to the crematorium. The gates opened onto a wide, wooded landscape with the crematorium itself settled in a glade which was effectively a huge, upturned bowl.

This too was crowded with onlookers, hundreds of them.

'Looks like a fuckin' pop concert,' Richie remarked and wiped his eyes.

***

Eventually it was over.

The humanist speaker – well drilled by Richie – had done a good job at describing Charlie's life without actually going into too much detail, other than to say he was 'a bit of a rogue.'

When the last mourners had filed out, Richie sat alone on the row of chairs at the front of the crematorium. He was in the centre of the row, looking blankly at the drawn, purple curtains covering the last journey his brother was ever going to make - along a conveyor belt and into a furnace hotter than hell. Beyond, Richie could hear the rumble of the gas flames that would disintegrate the body into a gritty, grey powder.

Roy sat behind Richie.

Two other men remained, seated further back, in different places.

Roy glanced over his shoulder at them. Their faces, like his, were stony and unemotional. Then he leaned over Richie's shoulder and whispered, 'We might have some help.'

Richie knew the men were there.

'I appreciate the gesture,' he said loudly without looking back, 'but I don't want anyone else getting involved. It's going to end bloody.'

His voice echoed away in this sacred place.

One of the two men glowered and stood up. He shot a terrible look at the back of Richie's head. Roy and the other man watched with scorn.

'What?' he said defensively. 'He doesn't want our help, so...' He started to flick a 'V' sign at the back of Richie's head but stopped himself as he remembered where he was.

Richie was now beaming from ear to ear. 'Arthur Bennett, only you – only you – would dare to have a joke at my brother's funeral.'

Arthur, who had begun to stalk out, stopped again and turned slowly. 'You know me, Richie, I'm either having a laugh or I'm fucking furious.'

'And we all thought you'd find a happy balance in your old age.'

Arthur snapped, gesticulating violently and screamed, now not caring where he was. 'Less of the fucking "old".'

Richie's head seemed to wind down into his neck at the outburst as if he expected a slap across the back of it. The other two men also shrank at the flare-up, when, just as suddenly as he had turned to ferocity, Arthur cooled instantly with an infectious grin.

'Relax, I was only joking.' He shook his head at the other men's seriousness.

'Good to see you, Arthur,' Richie said as he stood up and turned, smiling. He acknowledged the other man who was still seated. 'You too, Butch ... how's things?'

This other man was Desmond – Del – 'Butch' Kelly and like the three others, he was around the 70 year old mark He pulled a face. 'Bit boring since you left town last century, but I've got a feeling things might be changing.'

Richie nodded, took in the surroundings, enjoyed a momentary peace. He walked down the aisle and the three men clustered around him, all now serious.

'What's the score?' Arthur asked.

'There's at least six of them from what I saw on the video...' He paused, recalling the dreadful scenes, then he looked at each man and his voice became chilling as he said, 'I want to hear 'em screaming for their mothers before the end.'

'Sounds like fun,' Butch said and pouted with a shrug. 'I'll dig out my blades. So where do we find these bastards?'

'Ain't that simple, Butch,' Roy said. 'They're part of a bigger gang. There's loads of 'em.'

'And they've got youth on their side,' Richie warned. 'So we're gonna have to box clever.' He buttoned his jacket, undid it, fastened it – the mandatory three times.

Each man watched him, remembering the idiosyncrasy. None had seen it for a long time.

'But,' Richie announced, 'today is for Charlie ... tomorrow we go to war.'

TEN

Aaron lounged indolently on his chair behind the cheap dining table like an evil ruler cynically surveying his followers.

In this case they were three members of the sub-E2 gang, the young kids who did a lot of running around for the main gang, as well as watching and listening, in an effort to be fully enlisted.

They were 10, 11 and 12 years old respectively, one girl, two boys.

The lad in the middle of the trio pulled a wedge of cash out of his tracksuit bottom and offered it to Aaron who seemed almost repelled by the gesture.

'Fuck you doin' you little shit? I ain't involved.' He called across the room, 'Yo – ho!' and a pretty girl emerged from the bedroom, took the cash from the lad and counted it for Aaron.

'You guys steppin' up, yeah? Wanna get rich quick, yeah?' Aaron asked the three enthusiastically.

They nodded back just as enthusiastically. Aaron checked with the girl who had finished counting the cash. She nodded approvingly and shook the wad of money. Aaron reached under his chair and pulled out his stash box, took out some small bags of weed and handed them over to the young pretenders. 'Sell it, don' smoke it – now fuck off!'

They filed obediently out of the flat as DK stepped in.

Aaron sniffed. 'What you want?' he asked DK. His eyes were on the girl who had just counted the cash, lust in them. He was going to fuck her good.

'Aaron, someone's been asking questions about you?' DK said.

'That fucking bitch-cop?'

'Nah, some old geezer. Don't think he was a fed, looked more like a pensioner. He was talkin' to Lauren about that dead guy.'

Aaron stood up, rubbing his crotch. The girl watched him, lust in her eyes also. He started to steer her towards the bedroom and she went ahead willingly. As he passed DK, Aaron said, 'Sounds like we got to let people know to keep their mouths shut – or they the ones gonna be dead.'

***

The urn was an Ascot Black, solid brass, hand crafted with a polished black finish and a brass band encircling it.

It sat proudly on the bar of the Dover Castle.

Richie rotated it three times before placing a glass of Glenfiddich alongside it, Charlie's favourite tipple.

He glanced at the mourners in the pub, many of whom had earlier watched Charlie drive past. The RIP banner that had been outside was now pinned to the inside wall of the pub.

That said, the mood was relatively jovial, a lot of banter going on as Roy, Arthur and Butch reminisced about the old days, surrounded by a little coterie of ladies, most of whom were around their age, some younger, but all with big goo-goo eyes for the ageing gangsters, whose personalities seemed to fill the pub. Their numbers included Lizzy, but although she listened to the tall stories of derring-do and law evasion, her eyes constantly looked across to Richie who had taken up position by Charlie's urn. There was a blend of sadness and lust in her vision.

'What you thinking Lizzy?' Roy asked her, noting her glances at Richie.

'I think there's not many gents left in the world now.'

'A dying breed,' he agreed. 'I feel like I'm fighting a losing battle sometimes.'

The gaggle of ladies laughed, a sound like the tinkle of a bell, except for the one who had a terrible smoker's cough that made her rasp like a drain when she tried to laugh.

'They were good old days,' Lizzy said. 'This lot now, they don't know nothing about romance.'

'All piss and wind, the lot of 'em,' Arthur Bennett said forcefully. No one was certain if he was being angry or funny and they didn't know whether to say 'hear, hear' or chuckle.

Not one to notice anyone else's problems with him – self-awareness never having been one of his strong points – he grabbed his drink from the bar and downed it in one.

Giles, the landlord, offered a plate of nibbles to Butch. He selected something and tasted it, holding up his hand. 'No, don't tell me … liver?'

'Well spotted,' Giles applauded him. 'A new flavour.'

'Mind,' Butch said philosophically, 'I've cut enough of them out in my time, so I should know.' He smiled at Giles who blanched and had to control a retch. He did a quick exit to speak to two newly arrived customers, a man and a woman.

'I'm sorry, it's a private party tonight,' he said.

The woman nodded. 'I know. I'm looking for…'

'Detective Inspector Taylor,' Richie said from behind her. She swivelled at his voice.

'…Richie Archer,' she completed her own sentence.

'What can I do for you?' His gave Taylor's colleague DC Watts only a passing glance and effectively cut him out of the conversation.

'I'm sorry to interrupt…'

'But you did anyway.'

'We have no contact details for you, but we knew you'd be here, obviously.'

'Obviously.'

Around the pub, the chitchat had died down somewhat and all eyes were on this encounter.

Taylor genuinely had not wanted to interrupt what was essentially a wake, knowing how touchy people could be at such affairs, especially towards uninvited guests, particularly cops. But she had discreetly followed the hearse earlier, been utterly astounded by the sheer volume of people who had turned out to pay their respects to Charlie. She had also heard one or two … not so much rumours … but character assessments of Richie and what he was capable of doing, which is why she had decided to come and face him on his home turf, surrounded by his own people, to lay down the law. This was a psychological move on her part to demonstrate she was not afraid of him and hopefully gain some respect from him.

'Can we talk in private?' she asked.

Richie eyed Watts again who looked uncomfortable and vulnerable, not like his boss who came across as being quietly invincible.

'You and I can talk over here,' Richie said, indicating an empty alcove at the back of the room.

She nodded and stepped towards it. Watts set off to follow, but Butch slid across his path, leaving him no route to get past. Butch held out a platter of nibbles.

'These are pigs' ears, I think,' he said gruesomely. 'Very tasty.'

Taylor gave Watts a little shake of the head, then sat down opposite Richie in the alcove.

'How is the investigation going?'

'We're still doing house to house – but it's a closed shop around here,' she admitted.

'So, some things don't change?'

'Mr Archer.' Taylor coughed uncomfortably, coming to the point of her visit and reinforcing her next word by leaning on the table and looking straight into his eyes. 'I want to find the person responsible.'

'Good, so do I.' A smile played on his lips.

'That's the rumour I've heard.'

'Oh, tip my hat to you … you've clearly not lost the skill of putting your ear to the ground, even though what you hear is shit.'

'It's my job to hunt murderers, not yours.' She sat back. 'I understand your loss.'

'I'm not sure you do.'

'You'll have to take my word for it.'

'What do you know about loss?'

Taylor's nose twitched as she weighed up this question. Then she looked steadily at him with her green-flecked eyes and said, 'My husband was a detective in Peckham. Flying Squad. Good man. One day he left our house and never came back. Want to know why? Sure you do. He was a great, brave man and faced down some of the most hardened criminals in London – all after your time, admittedly. But you know what? He went out to buy a newspaper one morning when he was off duty and walked straight into an armed robbery not two hundred yards from our house. He died because he took a bullet in the head that should have, by rights, gone into the shopkeeper's head. And, know what?' she sniffled, only just controlling herself here. 'That robber was never caught and to this day I ask every suspect or witness or informant about it in some vain hope … because I will never, never, give up trying to find out who killed him.' She stopped sharply. 'He left me with a babe in arms, Mr Archer … I'm a widow who is trying to balance being a mother with a full time, pretty stressful job.'

Richie listened impassively. But in his chest his heart beat faster and in those moments of revelation, he began to like DI Susan Taylor.

'And what would really make my life tougher is if you were thinking of going on some vigilante rampage.'

'I'm not a vigilante, Mrs Taylor.'

They eyed each other.

'And I'm not after sympathy, either,' she said.

'I see that.'

'I respect your family matters to you and I am sorry for your loss, but I'm sure you understand why I want you back in Spain as soon as possible.'

'I am not a vigilante,' Richie restated.

Taylor nodded, got up, collected Watts who was still being encouraged to try even more outlandishly flavoured nibbles by Butch and headed for the door.

Butch, Arthur and Roy descended on Richie.

'What you tell her?' Butch asked, chewing on some kind of gristle.

'That I wasn't going to be a vigilante.'

'You're lying … right?' Roy said unsurely.

'There's a difference between being a vigilante and a … oh, shit, who am I kidding?' Richie admitted. 'Now, come on guys, let's spring my big brother from his cell and set him free.'

Richie pushed himself up, strode to the bar and grabbed Charlie's urn.

***

It was cold down on the river and all four men felt a shiver through to their bones. They were standing, exposed to the chill, on the landing pier that jutted into the Thames from Blasker Walk on the Isle of Dogs, between Greenwich Reach and Limehouse Reach.

Richie was holding the urn.

Butch wasn't greatly happy and he looked around warily. 'You sure this is a good idea? I mean, this place?'

'What's wrong with it? Charlie loved it round here when we were kids,' Richie said.

'And when he was older, if you know what I mean,' Butch said mysteriously.

From Richie's puzzled expression, Butch made it clear. 'Well let's just say he won't be the first person we've dumped in the water here … the tide, as I recall, is very cooperative around here.'

Roy cottoned on, adding, 'And this is where we dumped that shooter after killing…'

'After killing that cunt, McVey,' Arthur said, taking it up. He was instantly enraged by the literally dredged-up memory. 'I'd like to dig that skimming bastard out of his grave so I can shoot him again! A full cylinder wasn't enough for a twat like him, even if six did the job.'

'Arthur, Arthur,' Richie cut in, the intervention calming his friend. All four exchanged knowing looks and Richie said, 'It really is good to see you, gents.'

'Here's to the good times,' Butch said.

Richie looked at the urn. 'And the bad.'

There was a moment of reverie, then Arthur said, 'Fuck me, if only old lady Thames could talk.'

They laughed and Richie said, 'That's why this is the perfect place.'

He unscrewed the lid of the urn, tightened it, unscrewed it … three times, then raised it up, leaned over the pier railings and scattered the ashes with a whoosh into the air before they floated down to the surface of the river and hopped onto the outgoing tide.

'Be seein' you bruv.'

They watched in silence and then Roy pulled out a silver hipflask and passed it around. Each man took a sip and raised the flask to the memory of Charlie Archer.

***

It wasn't as if she was asleep. She had been lying awake for hours, almost as long as the man outside her house had been walking up and down the street until he plucked up the courage to knock.

She shot upright, her stomach tight.

Another knock.

Quickly she tiptoed to the bedroom window, peeked through and emitted a little gasp and a squeak. She grabbed her satin gown, slid into it and rushed down the stairs to answer the door.

***

'Richie,' Lizzy said, keeping the security chain on the door.

Suddenly his courage deserted him. 'I'm sorry, Lizzy, this is silly. I'm sorry to have disturbed you.' He made to turn away, but she almost slammed the door closed in her haste, slid the chain off and reopened it.

'Don't go … don't…'

He stopped, scratched his head and turned slowly. He was almost taken breathless by the vision of her, wrapped tight in the knee length satin dressing gown which showed the lower half of her bare legs and accentuated her generous breasts under which her arms were folded.

'I was hoping you'd come,' she said softly.

'I been out here three hours.'

She smiled – the smile of a woman who could have been forty years younger.

'I was wondering,' he said bashfully, 'if you wanted to make up for some lost time.'

Now she giggled, though deep inside something primal stirred. 'What?' she teased him, 'two OAPs going at it like hammer and tongs? I'm not even sure where everything goes

110

these days, whether it'll all work and what fits where … and,' here she gave him a significant look, 'whether we're both up to it.'

'I have all those thoughts too, Lizzy … but you know, as they say, where there's a will…' He held out his hand, opened it to reveal a pill resting on his palm.

'You'd better come in,' she said urgently.

***

Everything worked perfectly, much to the amazement of them both, and they revelled in the euphoria of laid-back, mature love making, and their age was no barrier. Afterwards they lay on their sides, facing each other, legs and arms wrapped around, talking quietly. They were not words of regret. Things happened, relationships came and went, they had missed each other because of the hand of fate and that's how it was. Now they were rejoicing in what time they had.

'Better late than never,' Lizzy said. 'I never thought I'd have Richie Archer in my bed.'

'It was wonderful.' He stroked her hair.

'Not bad for a couple of old crones,' she laughed prettily.

'Could show the youngsters a thing or two.'

'Not wrong there.' Lizzy crushed herself up to him and groaned with pleasure to find that the pill was still working its magic.

Later, they fell asleep in each other's arms.

Two hours after that, Richie awoke, eased his arm from underneath Lizzy's shoulders, sat up and began to get dressed. Lizzy woke groggily, reached out and touched his back, running her fingertips down his spine.

'Time to go to work,' he said.

'I know … be careful … please be careful.'

ELEVEN

From those early hours, the rest of that day was spent in furious activity.

Richie, Roy, Butch and Arthur zipped around the East End visiting various locations, unearthing contacts – or the sons and daughters of contacts long departed – that they hadn't spoken to for ages.

First on the agenda was use of a warehouse and this was sorted by Richie and Roy who found the ideal premises on the ground floor of a disused warehouse in Limehouse, within spitting distance of the Thames. Cash changed hands, no paperwork existed and a unit was rented for a week, no questions.

Butch and Arthur were the weapon and vehicle quartermasters. Within hours they had bought a beaten up old Transit van, with a sliding side door, for cash and all the requisite documentation (false), which they had driven through the shuttered doors of the unit and opened to reveal an arsenal of guns and other equipment.

The four of them eagerly went to work cleaning and testing the weapons, dry-firing the guns, and checking the state of the ammunition.

Everything seemed to be in good condition.

By evening, the four of them were sitting in the unit around a paraffin heater, exhausted by their labours and either sipping whisky or smoking.

They were like a group of cowboys huddled around a campfire, surrounded by darkness. It didn't help that in the darkness were dozens of mannequins or parts of mannequins – heads, legs, torsos – scattered around the unit which had once been a clothing storage unit. The presence of these body parts was unsettling, even for these four hardened men, a portent of things to come.

So far the conversation had been perfunctory, mainly about the day they'd had, the characters they'd met, who they trusted, who they didn't, the deals they'd done.

Once again, it was a little bit like old times and up to a point the chat was about avoiding the elephant in the room, the real reason why they were here.

Butch was the one who broached the subject. 'So...' he looked around, seeing the broken body parts and the place reminded him of a serial killer's lair, 'we have our cave ... now what?'

All eyes turned to Richie who thought about the question and said, 'I need to step into the belly of the whale.'

**

LONDON: 1988

Charlie Archer burst through the front door of the Dover Castle and staggered across to the bar, clutching and supporting his left arm with his right. He hoisted the arm onto the bar top and dropped it there, covered in the blood that had run all the way down from the bullet wound in his shoulder.

The landlord then, a man called Bert Wittering, ran over. Charlie grabbed his shirtfront, his eyes blazing with fury and pain.

'Close the place, close the place – now!' he growled into Wittering's face, his spittle covering the landlord's frightened face.

**

The Dover Castle was the favourite haunt and meeting place of the Archer brothers. It was an ideal location for them, within the centre of their turf but also slightly off the beaten track, with a steady, trustworthy clientele and a landlord pleased to make a bit of extra money by providing a meeting room on the first floor.

The pub had emptied quickly, no one even bothering to finish off their drinks, especially when Charlie peeled off his jacket and shirt to reveal the gash of the bullet wound which

113

had ripped its way across his shoulder like a jet fighter's trail having crash landed in a field. It was a messy gouge, but had not entered the shoulder joint, just ripped muscle – and Charlie had a lot of that.

He ran the forefinger of his right hand along the wound and satisfied himself that it wasn't as serious as it could have been.

'Phone,' he demanded of the landlord. Wittering brought it on its long coiled wire and placed it in front of Charlie who lifted the receiver and wedged it between his right shoulder and ear. Before dialling, he said to Wittering, 'Glenfiddich.'

***

Richie, Roy, Butch and Arthur were at the pub within twenty minutes, locking the door behind them.

Roy, Butch and Arthur took up positions by the windows, guns in their hands, whilst Richie and Charlie had a conflab at the bar as Wittering cleaned Charlie's wound for him, lacing it with Savlon before covering it with a dressing from the first aid kit.

'Shit hit the fan,' Charlie said, wincing as Wittering touched the burning wound accidentally with the top of the Savlon tube. 'It was a fucking set up.'

'Bastards,' hissed Richie. 'They gave us their word.'

'The word of Pat Corrigan and Billy Morgan ain't even worth a shit,' Charlie winced again. 'Thank fuck I saw it coming.'

It was a big fallout about turf and control, a simmering conflict that had been bubbling for months as the Archer gang preened and blustered against the Corrigan Clan and inevitably, it was going to end in war, despite the fact that the Archers were willing to negotiate, convinced there was enough for everyone out there, but some people always felt the need to expand.

The negotiations had been arranged to take place on neutral territory and be conducted under the auspices of a third party without any interest in the outcome. The choice of location was a club in Soho owned by a man who made a fortune from sex shops, and his name was Terry Richards.

The conditions were that Charlie went alone, as did Pat Corrigan, the leader of the clan. They were going to thrash out details of a ceasefire between the gangs as, already, four people had been shot dead by the factions and it looked as though the conflict was going to spiral out of control.

The two gangsters met at noon in the middle of Richards' sex club, at a table in the centre of the small, raised circular stage, one chair either side.

On their arrival, within five minutes of each other, they were frisked for weapons by one of Richards' minders and when declared clean, they took a seat opposite each other in an otherwise deserted premises.

'Well, this is convivial,' Corrigan began.

'Nothing associated with you is ever convivial,' Charlie responded.

Corrigan grinned. He was a long time operator, starting out from small beginnings in Peckham, expanding as he grew up and muscling in and taking over many other territories by violence and intimidation. It was rumoured that twenty bodies lay dead in his wake over the years. He did not negotiate – and now he wanted a very big chunk of the Archer patch in East London, north of the Thames.

'Still,' he said, 'it's good to talk, Charlie.'

'So let's talk.'

'Okay ... fact is I want to see the last of you and your fuck-wit brother in the East End. I want you to walk, and that is the basis of my negotiations: you can have your lives and I can have your businesses.'

Charlie leaned back. 'Seems there's going to be a long way to go before we reach a compromise.'

Corrigan leaned on the table. He had a pock-marked face and his complexion looked like a bad map of the moon. 'In my vocabulary there is no such word as compromise. I get what I want, end of story.' He grinned.

'But the word 'lying' clearly is in your dictionary.'

Corrigan nodded.

'So that's the end of the meeting?' Charlie asked.

'So it would seem,' Corrigan confirmed.

'Pointless, then?' Charlie said.

'Nah ... wouldn't go as far as to say that.' Corrigan's eyes narrowed.

Past his shoulder, Charlie caught sight of movement. The door to the gents' toilet opened slightly and Charlie cursed himself for ever believing the word of a rival. It would be the last time that ever happened.

With a swell of power, Charlie's chair shot back and simultaneously he upended the negotiating table, rose and drove it into Corrigan's gut, sending him sprawling across the stage. Charlie leapt off the low stage and sprinted for the exit which he managed to reach as Billy Morgan stepped out of the toilet and fired off two shots from his revolver. He was a long way from Charlie and revolvers are really only accurate over short distances, but he got lucky and one of the slugs tore the landing strip across Charlie's shoulder, spinning him around as he got to the door. Fortunately he was able to maintain his momentum to crash out through the door which was being guarded on the other side by Terry Richards, Mr Neutral.

'Cunt' Charlie said and swung wildly at Richards but missed as he staggered past and ran, loping and injured down the street.

Morgan and Corrigan emerged from the club and despite the street being busy, they set off after Charlie, guns drawn, and even fired off a couple of rounds, not caring about innocent passers-by.

Charlie managed to reach his car, a Peugeot 406, and make it back to the Dover Castle.

***

'I fucking hate being made to look like a naïve prick,' Charlie said. 'We should never have trusted them, never.'

'Calm down,' Richie said. He paced up and down three times. 'Let's think this through.'

'Nothing to think through ... like I said, it was a set up.'

'You think Terry Richards was in on it?' Richie asked. Charlie nodded. 'So he needs to be factored into the equation.'

'Boss!'

Richie turned. It was Roy calling from his position at one of the front windows of the pub.

'Jack Houghton's here … just pulled up.'

'Is he alone?'

'Seems to be.'

'Let him in … but be careful.'

'Fuck, that's all we need, the friggin' law,' Charlie moaned. 'Ow! Watch where you're putting that stuff,' he warned Wittering who had just finished the tube of Savlon.

Roy unlocked the front door and opened it without showing himself and allowed Houghton to edge sideways through the gap and enter. Then he closed the door and locked it.

Jack Houghton stood three steps inside the pub and took in the scenario. He was a large, powerful bear of a man with a bag of authoritative charisma that made him very dangerous indeed. He was a detective chief superintendent, one of the youngest in the Metropolitan Police and headed one of the capital's most elite crime fighting teams, dedicated to dismantling the gangs which had criminal strangleholds in the city. He was good at his job. He was also on the take from the Archers and had been since being a wet behind the ears woodentop.

Houghton strode over to the brothers, a grave look on his craggy face.

'What the fuck is going on?' he asked, saw Charlie's shoulder wound and flinched. 'It's like fucking Dodge City in Soho and you guys've been fingered as the culprits. So, like I said, what's going on?'

'Jack, you know what's going on,' Richie said placidly.

'Really? Fuckin' fill me in, then.'

Charlie rushed towards him. 'Be a fuckin' pleasure,' he said, raising a fist. Richie stopped him with a hand across his chest.

'This has gone too far,' Houghton said. 'It needs to stop, now.'

'That's what we intended,' Charlie said, settling back on his bar stool. 'But those bastards weren't up for it, now what do you think about that, copper?'

'What I think is this … Corrigan and his gang are dangerous, violent and stupid and they like killing people,

117

doesn't matter who. They're going to come for you now and if you don't get to them first, they'll have you.' His eyes blazed. 'And I won't be able to help you.'

Richie's right hand shot out and his fingers closed on Houghton's throat, squeezing tight. Despite his size – Houghton was physically larger than Richie – Richie had the power and mind-set and he slammed the detective up against the bar as Houghton fought to peel those fingers from his windpipe. Richie's face was close up to his as he growled, 'Then you'd better start doing what we pay you to do, and we'll do the rest.'

***

LONDON: Present day.

Apartment 1020. Richie had found it hard going walking up ten flights of stairs – the lift, of course, was not working – and he was quite breathless when he reached the tenth floor of the block and had to stop and lean on the walkway rail in order to settle down his lungs and heart, both of which felt tight in his chest. It had been a soulless climb, crunching on discarded needles like they were the husks of cockroaches, on other bits of broken glass and all manner of other litter.

'Horrible,' he said to himself, looking across the view, seeing the scars where the other tower blocks had once been, this one, the final one of the four already demolished, soon to join its compatriots as aggregate.

Breath back, heart rate normal, Richie made his way along the walkway to flat number 20. Before knocking he saw that the door was a complete mess with jemmy marks around the locks, the imprint of what looked like the circular head of a metal door-ram also around the locks, and new pieces of wood yet to be varnished that had obviously been fitted by a joiner to repair the splintered wood. The lock itself was clearly a new one, too.

Richie wondered how long it would take him to pick it.

He knocked three times in an unthreatening way.

There was some movement behind the door. Richie could sense himself being scrutinised through the security peep-hole before the door opened at couple of inches, the security chain still in place. One eye of a man looked out through the gap.

'Hello Jack, long time no see,' Richie said.

'Richie Archer?'

'The one and only, Jack … can I come in?'

The man hesitated, uncertain.

'You know I'll only kick it in. Be a shame to waste money on another new lock.'

The man grunted, closed the door, slid off the security chain then reopened the door and stood in front of Richie whose sharp eyes gave him the thrice over.

Richie had to admit, the intervening years had not been good for former Detective Chief Superintendent Jack Houghton, Met Police.

Richie remembered him as all brash and bollocks, one cocky, confident individual who towered over others and suffered no one gladly. That man had now gone to be replaced by a hunched over shell of what he used to be. And not only that, Richie noted, he had fear in his watery, grey eyes.

'I heard about Charlie,' Houghton said. 'Bad business.'

Richie nodded. Houghton turned, slightly off-balance, and went inside. Richie stepped through the door, closed it behind him, opened it, closed it, three times.

Taking in everything as he went, Richie followed the former cop to the lounge where Houghton slumped almost lifelessly into his armchair whilst Richie looked around, shocked at the wanton destruction that the recent visit from the E2 had had left behind, though of course he did not know it was E2 that had done this.

Houghton had managed to tidy out a corner of the room, but the rest remained trashed, graffiti on the walls, the smashed photos, the broken TV in the corner, the smashed screen reminding Richie of a huge mouth with jagged teeth.

'I don't like what you've done to the place, Jack,' Richie quipped.

'Fucking kids these days,' Houghton spat. 'No respect. They can't just take things, they've got to destroy things.' He picked up a broken photograph in a frame. He looked at it sadly, touched it, sighed. It was a picture of a pretty woman, taken many years before: his wife.

'That's why I'm here. I need your help, Jack.'

'Forget that,' he huffed. 'Those days are long gone.'

'I thought so, too, Jack, but yet here we are again.' Richie looked meaningfully around the room. 'What did the police say about all this? Did they even come and see you? Did you get your crime victim number?' he asked contemptuously.

Houghton grimaced and fidgeted uncomfortably on his chair.

It dawned on Richie. 'You haven't even called them to report it! Well that shows good faith in the old network.'

'It ain't that,' Houghton said. His voice was weary.

'It's a pointless exercise, you mean?' Richie said. Houghton could not look Richie in the eye. He went on, 'Ah, you can't bear the thought of them seeing how pathetic they'll all end up when the force spits them out the other side.'

Houghton's chest fell in a breath of defeat. He changed the subject. 'You're in good shape, Richie. Kept well.'

'It's the sun and the fresh food.'

'Should've gone myself when I had the chance,' Houghton said.

Richie's attitude changed at this, softening, more caring. 'You stayed for her.' His eyes fell to the cracked photograph in Houghton's fingers. 'And that was the right thing to do.'

'All the money I made on the side, all those deals we made, it all went on her care, you know? And for what?' His tone became bitter. 'Same result as if I'd done nothing.'

'You had no option - and we all got to die at some point.'

'It's always too soon for those we leave behind.'

Those words struck Richie. He glanced at other photos – Houghton's grandchildren. 'See them much?'

'When I can. They give me hope that the next generation aren't all animals.'

A silence descended as the two old acquaintances – friends, colleagues, mates, would have been incorrect words to describe their past relationship. Parasites, possibly, feeding off each other. It was certainly a symbiotic relationship, one in which each depended on the other.

But Richie hadn't come to reminisce or have a chinwag.

'I need some inside help, from your friends in blue.'

'What do you need?' Houghton said, knowing that the visit wasn't just social.

'Restrict the manpower on Charlie's murder investigation, for one thing.'

Houghton chuckled. 'I don't have to ask for that, Richie. It's probably already happened … they'll be at full stretch because there's probably half a dozen other murder inquiries running across London as we speak. The manpower to fully staff an investigation like we used to … thing of the past.'

'Okay, I'll have that.' What he really would like to have asked for was to get DI Taylor side-lined onto something else. She was a tenacious little bitch, he thought – and that was a complimentary viewpoint – and he could see she might be a problem for him. Richie guessed that was a request too far and the best thing he could do was just keep a couple of steps ahead of her, hence his next request. 'I need records for some toerags called Aaron and Maz.'

'Even if I agreed, who says they'd listen to me anyway?'

'I'm sure a former detective chief super still has some clout, some ears somewhere, even in the Met.'

'And what am I going to say?' Houghton began to distance himself. 'Here lads, fancy doing me a favour?'

'I don't give a flying fuck, Jack. What you say ain't my problem, just as long as you say it. I put an awful lot of money in your back pocket over the years, Jack.'

'And I kept you out of the nick. You and most of your lads. We all benefitted.'

'I think there was a bit more to it than that, Jack,' Richie said. 'Remember Billy Morgan? Pat Corrigan? Terry Richards? All dead.'

'Yeah,' Houghton sneered, 'and who took over their turf?'

'True enough, but not the point. I think, "Met Police Ordered Gangland Hits" is more of a headline even today, don't you? The bodies are still where we put them. I'll show you if you like. Just think of all the thousands of unsuspecting people who go to work in Canary Wharf every day … if only they knew what lies buried underneath their feet.' He winked.

***

LONDON: 1988.

Terry Richards looked with horror at his right hand which was skewered by a carving knife to the very same table at which, only hours earlier, Charlie Archer had been about to enter negotiations with Pat Corrigan. Richie had dragged Richards screaming from his office to the raised stage where Charlie had been waiting, pinned his arm down and his brother had driven the long blade through the back of Richards' hand and into the table.

'Now then,' Charlie said into his ear, 'I want the fucking truth.'

'I'm fuckin' tellin' ya,' Richards screamed, fear and agony mixed up inside him like a horrible cocktail. 'I didn't know, I didn't know.'

Richie circled the table three times.

'Your club … you were supposed to be the fucking chairman, the fucking facilitator,' Richie accused him, 'but truth was, you were with them, weren't you?'

'No … I swear on my…' Richards hesitated, not completely certain on whose life he should swear. In the end he said, 'Mother's life.'

'You fuckin' sleaze-bag of a hypocrite,' Charlie said. 'You beat the living crap out of your mother for ten quid and that was before you became her pimp.'

Richie stopped circling. He drew a weapon - a two-inch barrelled Smith & Wesson Detective Special. He shoved it hard against Richards' temple, cocked and un-cocked the weapon three times.

Richards went stiff, not knowing if he should look at his bleeding hand or try to see the gun at his head.

'Last chance, Terry,' Charlie said.

'What's it worth?'

'What's what worth?' Charlie asked.

122

'The truth,' Terry Richards said.

The brothers eyed themselves in amazement.

Charlie said, 'I think you've just told us the truth, just not in so many words.'

'Wha..? I haven't said a dickie-.'

Richie pulled the trigger. The hammer slammed down onto a hollow-pointed .38 bullet which entered Richards' brain just slightly above and to the right of his ear, spun wildly around like a coin trapped in a fast spin wash, then exited by making a jagged four inch diameter hole on the opposite side of his head.

***

LONDON: present day.

'I scratched your back, you scratched mine. That was the deal, Jack. Well now I've got another itch, Jack – a big one … and to be honest, I thought your lot would've welcomed a bit of help.'

'How do you make that out?'

'Well, on the face of it, this lot who killed Charlie and others like 'em are walking all over you and the East End.' He glanced around the trashed flat, making his point. 'It's embarrassing.'

Houghton seemed to rise in stature, his jaw clenched as if the sudden thought of revenge was very sweet. He looked into Richie's eyes and the two men understood each other.

'I'll see myself out,' Richie said.

TWELVE

Lizzy heard the deep rumble of the drum beat before she even got to the front door of her house, but thought nothing of it. She was still in a beautifully syrupy mess following the encounter with Richie which, beyond the purely physical pleasure (something she'd been certain would never be ignited again) – had had a major effect on her whole inner being, had brought her alive, put a spring in her step (who knew that cliché could be so true?) and almost made her feel like twirling all the way down her hallway as she collected her keys, handbag and open the front door in a state of euphoria.

But before opening the door she paused and got a grip. She asked herself if there could possibly be a future here to replace the missed past ... or was she jumping ahead of herself? Richie was a man she hadn't seen for many years, she had no idea what he had been doing in those years, what was happening in his personal life because there had been no time to discuss anything ... so perhaps she would have to tuck away any hopes and expectations, enjoy what had happened (which was great) and see how it all panned out.

Keep real, gal, she told herself ... then, even more realistically, she thought grimly that Richie might even go back to Spain in a casket.

Forcing that awful prospect from her mind, she unlocked the door and in so doing allowed the full force of the music she had heard to spill into her home.

It was coming from a car parked on the avenue right in front of her house. An old, black BMW, the kind of car she called a pimpmobile – fat tyres, blacked out windows, silver tyre trims.

As she stepped onto the front path and closed the door, she thought nothing of it. There were loads of cars around here like that. They were like an epidemic.

Then the music suddenly stopped.

Lizzy halted too.

The driver's window slid down to reveal a face covered by a plain, white mask that reminded her of the famous painting by Edvard Munch, The Scream, depicting a figure with an agonized expression. It was also similar to the protective masks worn by ice hockey goalkeepers.

Lizzy re-gripped her bag tightly, her first thought being she might be robbed.

Then the masked figure placed a finger across the mouth-hole of the mask – shhh – then using the same finger, in another unmistakeable gesture, sliced it across his throat. The warning was very, very clear.

The first two fingers of that hand, held in a 'V' shape, pointed at the eye holes in the mask and then at Lizzy.

I'm watching you!

The window slid back up, the face disappeared behind tinted glass, the thumping music restarted and the car skidded away from the kerb in a haze of blue smoke, leaving Lizzy terrified, her mood having been completely turned on its head within a matter of seconds.

Suddenly, she felt very vulnerable again.

***

Lizzy being Lizzy, her fear soon turned to anger and indignation and not long after she was in the Dover Castle, pacing furiously at having been threatened – literally – on her own doorstep.

Roy, Butch and Arthur were trying to calm her down, but even as a joint force, they did not have the necessary wherewithal to quell a woman's ire.

'The little shits ... thinkin' they can scare me ... they're not even real men...'

Having been summoned by Roy, Richie entered the pub, took in the situation and saw the distress on Lizzy.

'What's happened?' He crossed to her, stood in her path to prevent her from walking and took her arms gently, but firmly and looked into her eyes. 'Did they hurt you?'

She calmed her breathing and now she had the courage to speak directly to Richie, she said, 'You need … we need … to sort these … they're not people, they're not part of society…'

'Did they touch you? Physically hurt you in any way?'

'No, no, you don't understand, Richie. I've had enough. We've all had enough … everyone around here has. If you're going to go after these bastards, I want to help … we all want to help…'

Over to you Richie, he thought.

***

Lauren was in the kitchen, smiling as she texted Dean back. Nice boy/girl texts.

He had asked her if she was okay and if she'd like to meet up for a drink … a latte somewhere, maybe?

She sent him a text back. 'Sure.' She even added 'xx.'

It was lovely. He was lovely. This was how it should be. Soppy.

Then a text landed on her phone from a withheld number.

It was a photo. A frame-grab of Lauren bent over the wheelie-bin in the alleyway with a queue of E2 gang members behind her and her skirt hitched up above her waist. The faces of the gang had all been pixelated out.

The accompanying text read: 'Keep your mouth shut or it'll get filled by the E2.'

Lauren's happiness faded instantly.

***

DI Susan Taylor was still fuming with herself for having opened up to Richie Archer about her husband. She still wasn't sure why she had done it. To gain respect, credibility … not certain, but Richie had somehow drawn the response out of her by his manner and what she had said had seemed right in the moment but on reflection she felt it had diminished and weakened her and showed a little bit of unprofessionalism.

She drew up outside her house. It had been a hard day and not much had moved forward on the Archer murder but she was pretty exhausted and was glad to be home - a place of peace and safety, where the outside world could just fuck off. She took a few moments to reflect on her dead husband, shed a quiet tear or two before wiping her eyes and saying, 'Right, tea time.'

***

Lauren deleted the horrific text immediately, but jumped out of her skin when the front door of her house opened and her mother blundered in, carrying a brief case, papers and files which she dumped on the kitchen table in front of Lauren.

'Hi mum.'

'Hi, darling, how was your day?'

Lauren hid her shakiness. 'Same as always.'

Her mother kissed her on the head, sensing something amiss: that was the problem having a Detective Inspector for a mother – she saw through every smokescreen, especially this mother who worked on a Murder Investigation Team and was called Susan Taylor.

'You sure everything's okay, love? You've seemed a bit distant lately – and you've not really been out, either. Not ill, are you?' Taylor smiled. 'Or is it a lad?'

Lauren could literally have spewed her guts at that moment, but she covered her discomfort with a washed-out smile and a bit of bluster. 'No, mum, I'm not and it's not a lad. I'm just tired, that's all. Work, y'know?'

'Come on babe, I know you better than that … if something's bothering you, you know you can tell me. We always said no secrets … that's how it's always been between us.'

Lauren smiled genuinely this time. 'No secrets, honest. I'm fine, mum, really.'

'Hmm,' Taylor said doubtfully. 'I'm a copper, remember … I can sniff out when something's iffy.'

If only you did know, Lauren thought bleakly.

***

They were sitting on the balcony of Jack Houghton's flat watching the sun set over the East End. The new world of Canary Wharf glistened behind the old world of the East End, which had been called 'The Kingdom' back in Richie's heyday.

'Not quite the Med, is it?' Houghton said.

'Not quite … but things are what you make 'em,' Richie answered. 'It has its charm, its history.' He looked sideways at Houghton. They were sitting in cheap plastic fold-out chairs drinking cheap whisky. 'That's why it's worth fighting for.'

Houghton nodded. 'Speaking of fighting, I convinced an old colleague in the evidence room to make this disappear.'

From his pocket he pulled out a knuckleduster.

Richie recognised it straightaway. 'Charlie's.'

'Thought you might want it.'

Richie nodded thanks, took it, stroked it and pocketed it.

Houghton looked slyly at him. 'So what did happen, Richie?'

'You know I can't tell you that.'

**

LONDON: 1988

A war erupted following the violent death of Terry Richards. It lasted four months and cost too many lives. The police were under massive pressure from politicians and the media to bring an end to the violence but every cop knew that the only way it would end was if the gang leaders met their deaths in an untimely fashion.

It wasn't going to be Richie or Charlie Archer that met their maker, though.

They had lived rough for six weeks – 'going to the blankets' in Mafia parlance – bedding down in safe houses, grot-box hotels and brothels. Charlie killed two of Pat Corrigan's men and in retaliation Corrigan hit back with a double murder of two of the Archer's low-level runners who were not really involved in the dispute.

This elimination of almost non-combatants had enraged the brothers and they set about hunting down and destroying Corrigan and Morgan, but they were elusive and lucky prey.

It was Jack Houghton who stepped up to the mark.

He met the Archers in the back room of the Dover Castle.

'They'll be at Limehouse nick at nine o'clock tonight,' he informed them. 'It's a secret meeting … the Assistant Commissioner Crime has been making noises, as you know – because you two have ignored his requests – and he intends to do some banging heads together, threatening and negotiating with Corrigan and Morgan to try and end this fucking fiasco.'

The brothers exchanged a triumphant glance.

'They'll be arriving in a car driven by Ray Dryden and the meeting will be over in an hour. The AC is allowing them to park in the secure yard at the back of the nick … that said, I don't want a fucking Elliot Ness scenario when they drive out, y'know, machine-gunning the car?'

'We need to get to the car,' Charlie thought out loud. He looked at Houghton for an answer.

'What?' the detective squirmed.

'Get us hidden in the nick or in the back yard or whatever…' Charlie was on his feet, thinking. 'We exchange Dryden for one of us … what car are they gonna use?'

'Their black cab.'

'Fucking 'A',' Charlie said. 'Even better … and Dryden always wears that stupid cowboy hat, don't he? Easy for one of us to be him for five minutes.' He looked at Richie, excited.

'I'm up for it.'

Their eyes turned to Houghton. 'Shit,' he said despondently, 'I'll sort something.'

'This is the only way to end this thing,' Charlie assured him.

'Yeah, I know … kill the fuckers.'

No one even bothered to check through the stolen car that was towed into and left in the rear yard of Limehouse nick by a recovery vehicle and slotted in amongst the other stolen cars in the secure compound.

Had they done so, they would have discovered the curled up form of Charlie Archer in the boot. Through a jagged hole in the rusted bodywork he had a good view of the comings and goings of the yard, which also gave access to the basement floor of the police station.

Corrigan's personal black cab arrived on time: 8.55pm.

Ray Dryden parked it up and both Corrigan and Morgan climbed out to be greeted by the Assistant Commissioner and his lackey – in this instance, Detective Chief Superintendent Houghton – and led inside.

'Good man, Jack,' Charlie said.

Five minutes later, as expected, a uniformed constable emerged from the back door and approached the cab in which Dryden was listening to country & western music. The PC pointed and gestured politely, asking Dryden to reverse the cab back a few yards so as to keep access clear to the station doors. That, at least, was the story. The reality was that Houghton had realised that the cab was parked in full view of the CCTV cameras covering the nick entrance. He'd asked the innocent PC to ask Dryden to park further back on the pretext of access to the station. The position he moved to was out of range of the fixed camera over the door. When Dryden complied with the request – and why shouldn't he have done? – the PC gave him a thumbs up and went back inside, not realising the consequences.

Charlie gave Dryden a few moments to settle, then unfastened the boot lock and slithered out of the stolen car. Crouching low he moved from car to car until he sneaked up to Dryden's door, yanked it open and stuck a pistol to his head. From there he manoeuvred Dryden back to the boot of the stolen car, made him strip and climb in. Charlie then gaffer-taped his hands, feet and mouth – and shot him dead.

He pulled on Dryden's jacket – a suede leather cowboy thing with tassels down the sleeves, put on his cowboy hat and assumed Dryden's position behind the wheel of the cab.

Corrigan and Morgan came out forty minutes later and Charlie drew the cab in alongside them, keeping his face hidden under the shadow of the brim of the ten gallon hat.

Corrigan and Morgan climbed into the rear shouted, 'Home,' and settled back into the leather seat alongside each other to discuss the meeting.

Charlie could not hear a word, but he didn't care.

He selected 'lock' on the back doors and turned out of the station gate, initially heading towards Corrigan's manor.

It was too late for the mobsters when they noticed the change of direction. They banged on the dividing glass, screaming obscenities at the man they thought was their driver. That was until Charlie turned and revealed himself... and then they knew it was too late.

'Howdy partners,' Charlie said through the intercom. 'Where to? The gates of Hell?'

***

LONDON: present day.

Even now Richie could still feel his fingertip on the trigger of the Walther PPK as he unloaded a full magazine into Pat Corrigan and Billy Morgan as they sat trapped in the back of their own black cab, 'Hoist,' as he liked to say later, 'by their own petard.'

'Well, suppose it doesn't matter now,' Jack Houghton said, 'but I always wondered what happened to them.'

'Best you still don't know,' Richie said.

'I'm just sorry I couldn't keep the heat off you,' Houghton said. 'Out of my hands completely, that, especially with Ray the Cowboy's body in the back of that stolen car on police property ... even though he wasn't discovered until a week later when the smell gave him away. Up to that point it was thought he had set them up and done a runner.'

Richie laughed.

But it had got too hot for him and Houghton was running out of options to protect him. In the end the only thing he could do to save Richie and Charlie from a relentless police manhunt was to deflect evidence away from one of them, direct evidence at the other and then start to 'lose' that trail and screw up evidence 'accidentally'. But this meant one of them had to run. Richie went for it and, other than for an occasional secret foray back onto UK soil, had remained domiciled in Spain. He had been warned, though, that although the evidence against him was 'thin', he should stay there because if he returned there was every likelihood of a fresh investigation which Houghton could not control.

That was 25 years ago, but Charlie's death had meant an overt return, whatever the consequences.

'Do they still want me?' Richie said.

'Now? They wouldn't know where to start. For one thing the arrest warrants went missing and not only that there is literally nothing about you on police computers, other than your very old convictions. They would literally have to dig up the paperwork ... it'd be like going into Area 51.' Houghton paused. 'But that's not to say they won't, Richie. I've heard that DI Taylor is a bit of a Pit-Bull.'

'I'll bet she is ... anyway, enough of that. The past, as they say, is a different place ... what've you dug up for me?'

Houghton handed over a folder that had been propped next to his chair leg.

Richie peeled it open, closed it ... three times.

Houghton watched him. 'You still got your 'thing' then?'

'It's not a 'thing', it's a medical condition,' Richie corrected him as he extracted the papers.

'They didn't know that back then, did they?'

'Nah ... just thought I was mental.'

Houghton raised an eyebrow thinking that assessment was probably spot on, although he would have added 'and dangerous' to the diagnosis.

'Everything I got is in there,' he told Richie. 'That Aaron must have kept his nose clean as there wasn't anything on him. But there's an address for Maz – full name Wayne Mason – who is a typical gobshite of the highest order ... arrested for the manslaughter of a World War Two veteran last year, but the CPS screwed up the prosecution and he walked...'

Richie studied the arrogant mug shot of Maz, sneering down his nose at the camera lens. Richie wanted to punch him until he died there and then. But thoughtfully he said, 'He should pay for that.'

THIRTEEN

It was a house in Bethnal Green that once, maybe, had been majestic. It was detached, set in its own grounds, and in the late 18th century had belonged to the owner of a silk weaving mill before the decline of that industry in the area. It was also close to the pub in front of which two weavers accused of illegally cutting silk from looms were hanged in 1769.

The building went into rapid decay, very much in parallel to the surrounding area. It somehow survived intact and its use changed over the last hundred years. It became a doss house, a hotel, a brothel, then was deserted and only occupied by tramps and druggies, until the present owner bought it for almost nothing and converted it into a bed-sit, a dank unpleasant world with thin walls and rats.

It was here that the young man known as Maz resided.

He had spent a bit of time ensuring that his hovel was secure when he wasn't in residence but when he was at home it didn't matter so much because the other people who lived in the other flats steered clear of him and would not dare to intrude for fear of their lives.

Arthur and Butch spent a little time casing the joint but finally decided there wasn't really anything to case.

'Fucking lovely building,' Arthur said as they walked to the main door through a garden that had once been a pleasant retreat for a gentlemen, but was now overgrown with thorns and thick bushes.

'Ugh,' Butch responded.

They entered unopposed and their senses were hit by a combined stench of drains, shit and weed.

'Jeez, it reeks,' Arthur said, holding his nose.

'Yup.'

They knew Maz lived on the first floor so they trod carefully up the steps, having to avoid the turd on the fourth stair which could have been human, or not, and made it onto the landing.

Number six.

They walked along the corridor and paused outside the door.

There was a lot of noise coming from all the flats in the building. Somewhere there was a shrieking argument going on between two women, somewhere a baby crying, elsewhere the heavy beat of music; the sound emanating from number six was from gunfire and warfare.

Butch placed his hessian tool bag on the floor and unzipped it. He handed Arthur a claw-hammer and took out a short sword for himself. He also handed Arthur a draw-string pump-bag which had been slightly cut to be used as a hood. He had one for himself.

Arthur touched the door of the flat with the head of his hammer and pushed it open.

Maz and Leroy were sitting side-by-side on a beat up old sofa with their backs to the door as they faced an immense flat screen TV on which soldiers were massacring other soldiers, raking them with machine gun fire as the two lads played Call of Duty on the X-box. The volume was up deafeningly loud, dulling their senses and they were so engrossed in the battle that neither of them had any inkling of the danger that had just entered their lives. Each held a remote controller and they jumped each time they fired a shot and ducked instinctively as their characters on screen were shot at, and cheered when they made a kill.

On the screen it looked as though a group of Russian soldiers had been lined up to be executed.

Behind Maz and Leroy, Arthur and Butch shrugged, then stepped up silently to the back of the sofa, hoods ready, then in a simultaneous movement, they managed to prevent an further unnecessary killings on the screen.

***

Their world was now completely black, the pump-bags over their heads, the draw-strings pulled tight around their necks.

They fought and wriggled to break free from the heavy throne-like chairs to which their forearms and shins had been gaffer-taped. They wrestled and pulled at the tape, trying to tear free, but it was thick, powerful stuff and their efforts were useless and their shouts also useless because their mouths had also been taped.

Suddenly the hoods were yanked off and at last Maz and Leroy could see where they were – in the unit, the lighting subdued, and the limbs of the broken mannequins just visible in the shadows.

Their struggle ceased as they took in their surroundings and the people who had brought them to this place, then, in one movement, their heads turned in unison, their attention captured by a man who was holding a long, curved bladed knife known as a Kukri which he was sharpening on a hand held block with a 'shh-shh' noise.

Their heads came forwards and they focused on the man standing directly in front of them, a figure dressed in black – jacket, shirt, tie, shoes – as were the three other men with him.

Richie Archer was that man, his face hard and solemn.

'Hello lads … now you can make this easy, or we can make this hard. What's it to be?'

Richie stepped forwards and ripped the strips of gaffer tape from their mouths, ripping out the fine hair of their young men's moustaches and goatee beards with them.

'Dis is a fuckin' joke, right?' Leroy said. 'What's wiv the Reservoir Dogs shit look? That supposed to scare me? Dis is fucked up, man, you got me?'

Maz chipped in. 'Nah, man, it's fancy dress, they all come as a boy band.'

The two roared with laughter.

Richie and the others stood silent and expressionless as they were mocked.

Butch stopped sharpening his knife, a souvenir from his national service, given to him by a Ghurkha soldier, his pride and joy ever since. And like the Ghurkhas, Butch also believed that when it was drawn blood had to be spilled.

Then he started sharpening the blade again. 'Shh-shh,' – with long, slow, careful strokes of the block.

Maz stopped laughing and his face darkened with agitation. 'Right, you old cunt, untie me and I promise to do you last,' he ordered Richie, then started to struggle against the tape again, as did Leroy.

'You won't get out of that,' Richie said.

'Fuck you, fuck you,' Leroy said.

'Where can I find Aaron?' Richie asked simply.

'Fuck you, untie us you wanker,' Leroy responded, still struggling.

Just for a flash, Richie's laid-back approach wound up Arthur who screamed angrily at him, 'Maybe if you explained to the nice gentlemen why we're here?'

The boom of his angry voice silenced everyone around him for the moment until its echo died away. Butch had even stopped sharpening the Kukri, but then resumed with the terrifying, 'Shh-shh'.

Richie's expression did not change, other than to blink. He said, 'This is how it is … my brother was kicked to death recently and at least one of you was involved.'

Butch stopped sharpening and added, 'Or maybe both.'

Richie nodded. 'Maybe both.'

The sharpening resumed.

'And now one of you…' Richie said.

'Or both,' Arthur interjected comically.

'… Or both, are going to pay,' Richie went on. 'But not until I know who Aaron is or where I can find him.'

Leroy had given up struggling, but regarded Richie with pity. 'You got no idea of the shit that's gonna come down on you when we get outta here!' He screamed the last two words. 'Fucking untie us, now.'

Maz's face was dark and menacing as he said, 'You don't fuck with us, cunt. We're E2. Know what that means?'

Richie waited for the punchline.

'It means you're fucking dead!'

'Death doesn't scare me, boy. I've stared it in the face many times and won … as have my friends … which is why we're still here today.'

'We don't give a shit about you,' Leroy sneered, 'or your faggot friends.'

'Well you should … you should give a shit who we are …
I'm not going to give a history lesson, just suffice to say
history is what makes us what we are today.'

'You're just four old twats,' Maz said.

Richie's eyes became pools of molten steel as they focused
on Maz who, despite his bravado, shrank back into himself
underneath the look.

'Oh yes, we know you like killing old man, easy targets,
pensioners?'

It dawned on Maz what Richie meant. The memory made
him snort a laugh. 'Ha, that old fucker? He wouldn't give me
his medals, so he got what he deserved – and then I prized
them out of his arthritic fingers … but what I did to him ain't
even close to the pain I'm gonna inflict on you.'

Richie ignored him, then said, 'Maybe I will give you just a
taster history lesson after all. See this guy?' He indicated Roy
standing just to his left, a step behind. 'He used to torture
people. He was good at it, too. The best, actually. He's got this
uncanny knack of knowing when people are lying to him.'

'I'm fucking terrified,' Leroy mocked. 'Don't let him near
me, I might wet my pants.'

Roy grinned, taking this in good part …. like banter.
'Unfortunately, Leroy, you might not know it just at this
moment, but you are telling the truth … you'll learn soon
enough why.'

'Now that guy,' – Richie indicated Arthur – 'him, he was
what you'd call an enforcer. Trust me, you only cross him
once. Never, if you have any sense.'

'Okay, fuck the history lesson … cut us loose and I'll let
you live,' Maz said.

Roy stepped up close to him, studying him intently, then
declared, 'He's lying. He wants to kill us. I can tell.' He
smiled at Maz.

'Then finally, we get to Butch here,' Richie said,
introducing the last, but not least, of them.' Butch took a bow,
continued sharpening the blade, shh, shh … 'Want to know
why they call him 'Butch'?'

'Cos he looks like an old dog's arse?' Leroy quipped.

Maz and Arthur laughed at this, which Maz found disconcerting; he wasn't expecting to be sharing a joke with his captors. As Maz's laughter ceased, Arthur's continued, building up to a very scary crescendo, then stopping as though the sound had smashed into a brick wall.

Arthur's face became stone-like again as he glared malevolently at Maz.

'Wrong ... although his face does resemble a dog's arse,' Richie said.

'Oi!' Butch stopped sharpening, pretending to be offended.

Richie grinned, turned back to his captives. 'It's short for butcher. He can carve up a body in fifteen minutes, can't you Butch?'

Butch stepped forwards, flashing the Kukri. He sized up Leroy who quailed under the inspection. 'I reckon I could do you in twelve, fuck all meat on you. All nicely jointed.'

'He used to work in a mortuary, then became a real butcher,' Richie explained and dovetailed his fingers. 'Merge those skills plus certain skills he learned in a special services regiment and fuck me, what've you got?'

'This is supposed to scare us?' Maz said. 'Make us think you're hard men?'

'Ain't got no respect for the E2,' Leroy said jumping onto Maz's bandwagon. 'When I get out of here, I'll find ya and then we're gonna...'

'For fuck's sake – shut up,' Arthur's voice boomed.

Richie turned his back on Maz and Leroy and he looked at his three companions. His shoulders dropped and his eyes zipped across all three.

'I'm reading my boss's body language,' Roy said, 'and he doesn't seem too pleased.'

'They're just not getting it, are they?' Arthur said, disappointed. To Maz and Leroy he said, 'You're just not getting it, lads.'

'Could be a language thing,' Butch suggested. 'I mean, we speak English and they speak, I don't know ... gutter-shit, is how I'd describe it.'

Roy lit a cigarette and reflectively inhaled, then blew out a few perfect smoke rings which rose gently, then disintegrated.

He placed the cigarette into the corner of his mouth and with it hanging there, went to Maz and replaced the strip of gaffer tape across the lad's mouth, smoothing it out carefully so it stuck well.

Next to Maz, Leroy eyed the process.

Roy then stood back to check his work, took another drag of the cigarette so it burned bright red hot, then he took it out of his mouth and screwed the fiery tip hard into the centre of Maz's forehead with a sizzle. Maz tried to rear free, but Roy kept at his task until he pulled the cigarette away and then went nose-to-nose with Maz.

'Now do I have your attention?'

Maz felt as though a soldering iron had been dug into his forehead. He nodded frantically.

'Were you there when my mate got done?' Roy asked him slowly.

Maz shook his head.

Roy almost tutted. 'Ah, you see – actually – I don't even have to rely on my innate ability to spot a liar.'

He glanced at Arthur who, without having to be told, stepped in from the side and drove a half-brick sized fist into Maz's temple, a crunching, hard blow, delivered with power and accuracy. If the impact had been recorded on a slow motion camera, Maz's whole head would have been seen to distort and shudder.

Maz could not hold up his head, which drooped loosely.

'You dim fucker,' Roy said to him. 'We've seen the video with you there, you fucking idiot.'

Arthur massaged his fist. The blow had hurt him too, but he wasn't showing it.

'I don't know why this generation spend so much time putting themselves on the internet, doing stupid fucking things,' Butch commented.

Arthur continued to massage his knuckles whilst he talked about the kids of today. 'It's those reality TV shows. Everyone wants to be famous.' Then suddenly in one of his famous rages, he snarled at Maz, 'You wanna be famous? Live fast, die young? Have a fucked-up corpse … courtesy of me?' His face had become ugly.

Maz shook his head, the cigarette burn on his head still smouldering painfully, and he could smell his own flesh. His face was contorted in agony. When Arthur had hit it, Maz had felt something crunch and grate and as he ran his tongue around the inside of his mouth he could taste salty blood, feel loose teeth. He was afraid now and all his bluster and contempt for these men in black had gone with a cigarette burn and a punch.

'Technically it'll be me that 'fucks-up' your corpse,' Butch corrected Arthur, raising the finely honed blade of the Kukri.

Maz felt very poorly.

Roy turned his attention to Leroy and gave him a fatherly smile. 'So, he's unable to talk now, it's your turn.' He steepled his fingers and for a very fleeting moment he could have been a kindly vicar. 'Where can we find Aaron?'

***

Aaron was, in fact, in his flat in his tower block, laid out on a stolen sun lounger on the balcony, looking curiously at his smartphone.

Inside, a young girl wearing headphones was crashed out on the sofa, whilst JP and DK were slouched on other chairs, idly texting or surfing the net on their phones.

Aaron sat up feeling annoyed and jittery. 'Where the fuck is Maz?' he called into the flat. If there was one rule for the E2, it was keep in touch.

'I bet he's out with some skanky bitch,' DK called back.

'Try him again, JP, and you call Leroy.' Aaron looked out across the view. 'Something's wrong … feel it in my piss.'

'Feds?' DK suggested.

'Nah, we'd have heard.'

JP found Maz's number, DK found Leroy's, and they pressed dial simultaneously.

***

Not too far away in a shit-hole bedsit in Bethnal Green, Maz's X-box was still running the warfare game, the huge TV still on, lots of shooting and screaming taking place.

On the wonky coffee table in front of the sofa were the two wireless remote controls and two smartphones which both began to buzz together.

***

Aaron heaved himself off his lounger and stood by the balcony window, watching DK and JP make their calls.

JP took his phone away from his ear and shook his head. 'Nothin.'

Ominously, DK did the same, said 'Nothing.' Then she went on, 'We got 'nuff enemies and most of 'em would take us off.'

'A war?' Aaron was not convinced. 'Shit, ain't no one in these ends got the stones to take us on … we like hunting dogs.'

'How 'bout the East Europeans, man? Dey spring up everywhere, real quick,' DK said.

JP put his phone back to his ear and said, 'Yo, Maz, man, call me … soon as,' onto Maz's ansaphone.

DK continued about the Rumanian gangs she had encountered. 'They fuckin' crazy.' Then, with dawning realisation, she said, 'If they got Leroy and Maz, what if they come after you and me … us?'

'Think we'd have heard something, but if someone's fucking with us, we gotta find 'em and we gotta crush 'em.' Urgently Aaron said to DK, 'You get everyone onto it, you got me? And you,' he said to JP, 'get everyone tight, no street corner stuff until we got this sorted.'

JP could not hide his pissed-off expression.

'Hey, JP, you work for me,' Aaron told him. 'I tell you not to be dealin', you don't be fuckin' dealing.'

'Yeah, but…'

'Yeah but fuckin' what? You think I give a fuck about your opinion? You telling me how to do this thing?'

'I just wanna shift weed,' JP whined.

141

'No. I don't want no-one else going missing, right? And find my bros.'

DK's mind had been whirring and she had another epiphany of sorts. She sat upright. 'Fuck, man, what if it's that old guy I saw Lauren talking to?'

Aaron looked at her as if she'd lost her mind. 'An' how the fuck an old man gonna get my boys? Nah, can't be some nearly dead doing this.'

FOURTEEN

'I ain't tellin' you shit.'

'Good. Just how I like it.'

Roy backed off and picked up a holdall, then stood in front of Leroy, still smiling … but the trusting vicar look had gone and was replaced by the monster at the opposite end of the holy spectrum.

Leroy glanced worriedly at the bag, then at Roy. 'What you gonna do?'

Roy placed the bag in front of Maz's feet. It rattled metallically as it settled and Maz, though still groggy from Arthur's punch, looked on horrified.

'Hold on a minute,' Arthur cut in.

Everyone turned to look at him. He walked forward, tearing a strip of gaffer tape from a roll, then stuck it hard across Leroy's mouth, firming it flat with his thumbs.

'His mouth was getting on my tits,' Arthur explained apologetically. To Leroy, he said, 'Now listen to the nice gentleman.' He reversed away, wagging an admonishing finger at Leroy.

Roy leaned in close to Leroy, but pointed to Richie.

'We're upset because you and your mates killed his brother, so he wants to know who else was involved and,' he nodded as he chatted, 'one way or another you're gonna tell…'

Leroy glared defiantly at him, still unafraid, although the mask was slipping just a little.

Roy reached into the bag and extracted a claw hammer and two six-inch nails.

Without a further word, he moved quickly, hammering one of the nails through the back of Maz's left hand all the way through flesh and bone into the arm of the wooden chair, which explained why both Maz and Leroy had been so carefully taped to the chairs. It was all in the planning.

Maz jerked wildly, arching up his spine as if he had been jabbed by a cow-prod. Behind the gaffer tape over his mouth, he screamed but the sound was muted and more horrible for being so.

'That was for the war veteran you murdered,' Roy said. 'The one whose medals you had to pry out of his fingers. Not so fucking funny now, is it?'

As quickly as he had done the first one, he moved slightly and hammered the second nail into the back of Maz's right hand, pinning it to the chair arm.

Maz's muted screams were pitiful, but his pain intense.

'And I'm going to keep nailing this vermin to the chair unless you tell us what we need to know,' Roy informed Leroy.

'And you will tell us,' Butch assured him. 'So is it going to be now, or later?'

Leroy shook his head, his nostrils flaring, sweat cascading down his face.

'No?' Butch said. He looked at Maz. 'Nice mate you got.'

Maz was writhing in pain, each tiny movement making the rust encrusted nails rub harshly against the nerve endings in his hands, sending red hot shots of agony up his arms.

Roy put the claw hammer back into the bag and took out an old fashioned hand drill with a drill-bit already fitted. He held it up for Maz to see and slowly rotated the handle that turned the gear that rotated the chuck.

'You ever seen one of these?' he asked. 'It's called an egg-beater, and you can see why. Bloody antique … took ages … people really had to be held down tight … I tell ya, you have no idea just how hard it is to penetrate bone … but this is how we used to do it, the old way.' He looked misty-eyed for a moment, then pulled himself together with a little sigh at the memory. He shrugged, put the drill back into the bag and Maz exhaled in relief until he constricted up again as Roy pulled out a modern cordless drill which he displayed for Maz. 'But this – this is the new way.'

He tightened the chuck with his hand. Slotted into it and ready was a thin drill bit with a tiny point on the end, the type used for drilling holes into metal.

Roy was being conversational now. 'Talking about old ways,' he turned to Richie who was watching blankly, 'remember that time I sawed that bloke's leg off with a Tenon saw?' Richie nodded. 'Christ that was fun … anyway…' He squeezed the trigger of the drill and the electric motor shrieked as the drill spun.

Maz's eyes widened as Roy knelt down in front of him, pulled up his right tracksuit bottom pant leg, exposing the lower section of Maz's leg, from the knee down. Roy sized it up, running his hand up and down Maz's shinbone, squeezing his calf muscle, making him flinch. At the same time he was pulling and releasing the drill trigger.

Then he grabbed the shin tight, placed the pointed tip of the drill against the bone, then squeezed the trigger and drilled a hole into Maz's shin.

Maz emitted a horrifying, muffled scream, writhed and jerked as Roy ran the whole length of the drill into his legs, then extracted it with a thin squirt of blood from the hole.

Maz slumped in a faint.

***

Aaron was flicking crossly through his contacts list on his phone. He was beginning to get extremely agitated.

Then he realised. 'And Dean, yeah – where the fuck is he?'

JP said, 'I'm on it.' He found Dean's number on his phone and dialled.

***

They were huddled together on a two-seater sofa in one corner of a Starbucks café just off the E2 patch down near the Tower of London, two innocent kids on a date, sipping iced Mochas with lots of cream and marshmallows, having fun, giggling.

There was no pressure here, except when Dean's phone buzzed and he pulled a face at Lauren as he got it out and looked at it.

'I better answer,' he said apologetically, swiping the screen. 'It's JP.'

'Who you with?' JP barked.

Dean's eye flickered guiltily at Lauren. 'Er, no one … what you mean?'

'Y'seen Leroy or Maz in the last few hours?'

'No.'

'Then you fuckin' get on the street, ask questions … Aaron doing his nut in … we got to find 'em.'

JP ended the call.

Dean frowned and looked at Lauren who made his heart skip. She looked so utterly gorgeous and angelic and was being the real girl he knew existed under the brash exterior she'd invented for Aaron to become accepted by him.

'Don't tell me, you got to go?' she said.

'I ain't got to, but they want me to.'

'So … you gonna do what they want, or finish the drink?'

Dean hesitated: the million dollar question.

'I want to stay here.'

Lauren smiled. Her hand moved across to his and their fingertips touched.

'I mean … it's a wicked Mocha.'

He grinned at her and she gasped a laugh … and anyone not knowing them, just seeing them, would have thought they looked great together.

***

Maz had not regained consciousness. His head lolled loosely on his chest. The blood flow from the nails hammered through his hands had stopped and begun to coagulate. The drill hole in his in his shin dribbled a constant flow, pooling in his trainer.

Richie stood back from proceedings, still, silent, a brooding presence, his anger growing inside himself.

Roy pulled out a small vial of smelling salts from his pocket, flipped the cap and held the vile smelling, ammonium based compound under Maz's nose, the vapour instantly invading his nostrils, jolting him awake, but disorientated.

146

Roy held his head still and looked into his glazed, blood shot eyes. 'Sorry, son, but you got to be awake for this or it's kind of a waste of time.'

Tears flowed down the lad's face.

Then a sound - click.

All eyes spun to Richie who now had a sawn-off shotgun in his hands, loading, re-loading it.

'Another history lesson, boys,' he announced. 'But this time it's about a personal journey – your journey. All the bad things you have ever done in your lives have led to this terrible moment. It's called retribution.' He took a step towards the pair, loaded, unloaded the weapon. 'Karma.' Another step, another reload. 'Payback.' Another step, the third and final reload. 'Fate.'

Then he was standing directly in front of them, the shotgun slung almost casually over his right shoulder. He looked like a Colossus. Tall, broad, commanding … murderously dangerous.

'But I'm willing to stop all this … I'm willing to forgive … if you tell me where I can find Aaron.'

Leroy eyeballed him meaningfully, nodding.

Roy tore the tape from his mouth.

'L … look, I was there,' Leroy stammered. 'Okay? But I didn't do anything … honest. I didn't touch the bloke, your brother.'

'Where does Aaron live?'

'I don't know, I swear I don't … I never been there.'

'Lying! I can smell it,' Roy said.

Richie sighed.

Roy fired up the drill again and drilled into Maz's other leg.

'You see,' Richie said to Leroy. 'He can always tell when someone's lying.'

'It's a gift,' Roy said, standing upright.

Richie shrugged at Leroy: decision time.

Bravely he had a few more moments of internal struggle then said, 'Fuck, fuck, okay. If you let me go, I'll bring him to you … like a trap, whatever.'

Roy's eyes rolled in their sockets. 'That's an even bigger lie.'

Arthur erupted with anger. 'Drop your mates in it? Fucking Judas!' he scolded Leroy, who clearly could not win either way.

'You want me to start cutting?' Butch asked. He held up the Kukri, now sharpened to his satisfaction.

Richie and Leroy were still eye to eye.

'Let 'em go,' Richie relented, to the surprise of the others.

'What?' Butch screeched in disappointment. 'For fuck's sake, Richie.'

'I said let 'em go … they're just kids.'

'I swear I won't say nothing to no one,' Leroy promised desperately.

Roy bent in close to him, smelling if he was lying or not.

Leroy babbled on, unable to believe his good fortune – that these stupid old fuckers actually believed that he, Leroy, was going to lead Aaron to them. He didn't want to take any chances at that point and continued to try and convince them of his honesty. 'Tell me where you want to bring him and I'll do it, then I'll vanish, I swear.'

'Untie him,' Richie said.

'This is a mistake, Richie,' Roy said dubiously. 'This little shit'll grass on us.'

'I won't, man, I swear I won't.'

'Do it,' Richie said.

With a heave of reluctance Butch placed the Kukri down on the floor, took out a smaller knife and began to cut away the gaffer tape that held Leroy to the chair.

'You say a word to anyone or I even get a sniff of you around here again, you're history – got it?' Richie warned Leroy.

'Yeah, yeah, man,' he said, but thought, 'Dim wankers.'

At the last thread of tape was cut away, Leroy leapt forwards, bundled Butch out of the way and in a flowing, fast movement he scooped up the Kukri and with a murderous scream he lunged at Richie, the fine blade slicing through the air, intending to cut Richie's face off.

But before Leroy could do it, Richie had swung the shotgun down from his shoulder and fired at almost point blank range into Leroy's chest, tearing a huge, jagged tunnel right through

148

his slim body, destroying his heart and lungs and spine. The blast exited out of his back, leaving a gaping hole. Leroy crashed backwards and the Kukri spun harmlessly out of his hand and was caught expertly by Butch.

The four friends gathered around his body like pallbearers.

'I told you he was lying,' Roy said.

'And I believed you, like I always do,' Richie assured him, 'but I've never killed anyone when they've been tied up. It's unfair.'

For a moment all four retained their serious, funereal faces, then all cracked up laughing.

'What about the veteran killer?' Roy asked Richie, nodding at Maz's unmoving body.

Roy jerked his head at Butch who checked Maz for a pulse in his neck. It was there, but weak.

'Still alive.'

'See to it,' Richie told him.

Butch nodded and withdrew a stiletto knife out of his jacket. He found the exact spot, then with an almost gentle thrust, slid the fine blade deep into Maz's chest, into his heart, then extracted it.

'Let's call it a night,' Richie said.

FIFTEEN

Richie was sifting through some sheets of paper, computer printouts and photographs. He was sitting in Lizzy's lounge, a cup of tea by his side and Lizzy herself sitting opposite, feeding the sheets to him.

He stopped at one in particular.

'This 'JP' lad looks to be well connected,' he said and raised his eyes to Lizzy.

'In more ways than one ... he shares friends links with some of the names we've talked about, he's on Twitter and Facebook and some other less well known social media sites, but I can't find no one called Aaron or anything similar in these groups.'

'This is where you got all this?' Richie said, waving the papers.

'Yeah, social media sites ... you just got to know where to look ... it's easy when you get going.'

'Seems you're a bit on an expert with all this computer stuff then?' Richie complimented her and took a sip of his tea.

Lizzy threw her head back and laughed prettily, exposing her fine throat. 'Just a nosy cow. It gives me something to do, y'know? I don't get out as much as I'd like because ... well, you know the area.'

'Perhaps I can do something about that?' Richie suggested.

Obviously not knowing exactly what he had done so far, Lizzy said, 'I think you already have. There's a different mood with you being around.'

'Hey – nothing like a good funeral, eh?' he said cheekily.

'I didn't mean it like that,' she said sternly. Her eyes played over him and her chest filled with emotion. 'I used to have a massive crush on you, y'know,' she spilled the beans.

'I think we've established that.' He smiled at the memory of Lizzy, Viagra, an erection that would not go away and some amazing moments. 'You should have said.'

'Back then? No, no, no.'

'Why not?'

'You wouldn't even have looked at me. I was plain Jane as anything compared to the floozies you had on your arm.'

'All for show ... tits, arses and teeth, and complications, if you'll forgive the French.'

Once again their conversation went on pause as their eyes tried to work each other out. Lizzy gasped as she thought he was about to say something profound and life-changing. It didn't come. Instead, he rolled his watch around his wrist three times.

She watched this, frowning, 'So what is going on with you?'

He shook his head. 'Just getting the lay of the land for now.' He held up the printouts. 'This lot will really help ... anyway, I'd better…'

He stood up, as did Lizzy. It was an awkward moment, both now not daring to look at each other.

'If I find anything else, or you need me to do anything…' Her voice wavered.

'Yeah, course,' he nodded. 'Thanks, Lizzy ... er, listen ... do you fancy going out one night ... something to eat?' he asked, feeling like a teenager. She seemed to be caught off guard and he misread her look of consternation. 'It's okay, I shouldn't have asked.'

'No.' She touched his arm. 'Maybe do things the right way round?'

'You mean a date and then bed?' he grinned wolfishly.

'Maybe ... that said, I am so glad you came around the other night.'

'I needed it.'

'And so did I.'

'Meal then?'

She nodded. 'Meal.'

'Great ... once I've sorted a few things I'll figure something out ... and you must wear something red ... I remember that dress you used to wear. Stunning.'

She gasped, then giggled, then she was serious. 'Can I ask you a question, Richie Archer?'

'Course, darling.'

'Do you think it's ever too late to love?'

'No, no I don't.'

***

'This is particularly nice ... I'm sure you would look marvellous in it,' Lauren said genuinely to the lady who had been in the shop for over an hour now and was starting to drive her mad. She shepherded her gently towards the fitting rooms and breathed a sigh of relief as the lady went in with the dress, but the sigh stopped abruptly in her throat when she turned and saw Richie Archer behind her, admiring a red dress which he hung back on the rack.

'Hello, Lauren,' he said ominously.

Panic set in. 'Why are you here – again?'

Richie blinked. 'I'm not going to stop until I find the one responsible, Lauren. I'm a man of my word.' From inside his jacket he pulled out the sheaf of printouts Lizzy had given him. His voice was a little warmer when he said, 'Just wondering if you know any of these people.'

'I can't.' She did not even glance at them. 'They've threatened me and I am sorry, but I can't help you anymore.'

She set off. He caught her arm. 'Am I going to have to chase you through the store again?'

She wilted.

'Lauren, I'll let you into a little secret about threats and blackmail – and I have a thorough knowledge of the subject ... the sooner you find an exit, the sooner you find a solution, the sooner you get your life back.'

With a desperation he hadn't seen before in her, she said, 'They've got horrible pictures of me. I am so ashamed,' she went on, tears forming in her eyes. 'It's not even who I am, it's who I thought I should be, but I was so wrong ... the whole thing could ruin me.'

'And that's what they're relying on – your fear. It won't ever stop, Lauren. They'll keep turning the thumbscrews.' He gave a curt laugh. 'I used to do this for a living, so trust me. Help me and I help you.' She dithered, visibly trembled. Richie touched her arm tenderly. 'I have a daughter, older than you but she's all I've got and if something should ever…' He could not bring himself to think about it.

'I get it.'

'Let me remove these people from your life.'

'Shit, shit, shit,' she said, her mind in turmoil as she fought to reach a decision. Then she looked him directly in the eye and saw he meant his words. She nodded.

'Thank you, Lauren.' He offered her his hand. 'Friends?'

With a deep breath, she took it and they shook. 'Friends.'

'Okay.' Richie gave a little laugh. 'First thing, then, now we are friends … I don't want to keep scaring you at work, would you prefer it if I called you from now on?'

Lauren chuckled and pulled out her phone. 'What's your number?'

'I don't have one.'

'What do you mean, you ain't got a mobile phone?'

Richie shook his head. Lauren was amazed and slightly delighted. She smiled, grabbed the printouts and wrote down her number on one.

'Old school,' Lauren said.

'Less of the old,' he said. 'Now, they might have pictures of you,' – he did not want to tell her that he'd seen them – 'well, I've got pictures of them, too.'

Lauren sifted through the printouts, pausing long enough on Dean's photograph which was amongst them for Richie to notice.

'Was he there that night?'

'He had nothing to do with it, I swear.' She turned the page and JP looked up at her. 'But he was there.'

'Good … you know where he lives?'

'No, but I heard he serves up – y'know, deals weed – at the Grave End multi-storey car park…'

'What the hell are you doing here?'

They both looked up to see DI Susan Taylor marching towards them.

'DI Taylor,' Richie said smoothly.

'Mum!' Lauren said.

Richie wasn't fazed by Taylor's sudden appearance; good cops were always turning up in the most surprising and uncomfortable places. What did take him aback was Lauren's exclamation. Taylor was her mother.

Taylor stood between Lauren and Richie who surreptitiously concealed the printouts.

'I was looking for a red dress,' Richie continued, 'but haven't seen anything I like so far.'

'You stay away from my daughter.'

'I honestly had no idea this young lady was your daughter, although I do now see the family resemblance.' He looked at Lauren. 'Thank you for your advice,' he said.

He turned and walked away, bemused by this turn of events but also recalling the first time he had met Lauren and the feeling of knowing her somehow. He just hadn't slotted the pieces together, until now.

The two ladies watched him leave the shop without a backwards glance.

'Are you okay?' Taylor asked.

'Yeah, course I am. I'm fine, it was nothing … he was just a customer.'

Taylor blew out her cheeks as she exhaled with relief. 'Okay … ready for that lunch?'

***

The car park was his designated trading patch. Any incursions by others would be met with extreme violence and that was understood by everyone in the area.

Grave End car park belonged to JP.

He did a good, creditable business in the multi-storey car park with many dark places for exchanges to take place.

He dealt mostly in weed which was always popular in the East End. Other drugs rose and fell in popularity but good quality weed from a trusted supplier always had a ready market.

From his weekly sales he tipped over, usually, about £300 to Aaron (who was his supplier) and the rest he kept for himself, usually about the same amount. It was a good life and one JP was not about to jeopardise, which is why he was dealing that night going against Aaron's explicit orders. JP knew he had to keep his presence there, otherwise someone else would move in.

Grave End was also still a working car park, well used by the public during the day, less so in the evenings and night time, which was JP's main dealing time. Usually he didn't bother to look at members of the public. They were from a different world and he did not want any crossover – unless opportunity presented itself.

That evening the car park was quiet, almost deserted as JP skimmed around it on his BMX, waiting for business.

He'd already done a couple of hundred's worth and expected to double that before the night was over.

Very few cars were parked up and, as usual, JP ignored them. Stealing from them could complicate things if the cops were called and then turned up. All he wanted was simplicity, especially in view of the so far unexplained 'disappearance' of Maz and Leroy. Not that JP suspected anything was really wrong. He thought that they were both probably with girls, getting their heads fucked and that Aaron was being paranoid.

Still, that said, JP was never one to look a gift horse in the mouth and although he did like to keep his dealing and other criminal activity separate, an easy target was an easy target.

He was on the top floor of the car park watching the sun set, long shadows and an air conditioning vent keeping him well hidden.

There were two cars on the roof. One parked in the middle, one in the far corner.

JP heard the hiss of the lift arrive, saw the doors open wide and to his delight a doddery old man stepped unsteadily out onto the concrete roof. He was bent over double, clutching a bag of shopping, really struggling with it as he shuffled towards the car in the middle.

JP smiled: just his kind of victim – a hit and run.

He emerged from the shadows on the BMX, riding hard, pulling his hood over his head and wrapping a scarf around his face. As the man reached the boot of the car and fumbled for

155

his keys, he dropped the shopping bag which burst as it smacked onto the floor, tins of beans and peas rolling around, sending the old guy into a confused tizzy.

JP raced up at him and screamed, 'Oi! Fucking wallet now, you old fuck.'

The old man stood upright and turned slowly to the sound of the voice, but he did not have a set of car keys in his hand, instead he brandished a Kukri.

'Who you calling old?' Butch demanded.

JP skidded sideways, the bike almost losing grip on the shiny surface. Suddenly the headlights of the only other car on the rooftop came on full beam and the engine started with a roar as the Singer Gazelle's finely tuned twin carburettors spat fuel into the 1725cc engine which, old though it was, ran like a dream.

Roy was at the wheel.

JP instantly realised he had been set up, lured into a trap.

He shot past Butch, narrowly missing the swish of the Kukri, and pedalled furiously towards the exit ramp.

Roy screeched alongside Butch, who had flipped the blade of the knife in between his thumb and forefinger with the intention of throwing it at JP's back, even though it was not a true throwing knife.

'We need him alive,' Roy screamed.

Butch scowled. It was a very long time since he had thrown a blade in anger; these days it was all darts.

'I ain't got dementia,' he said as he jumped in alongside Roy. 'I was aiming for his back wheel.'

As Butch's door closed, Roy slammed his foot on the accelerator and went after JP who had already reached the top of the corkscrew-like ramp.

It was a tight, narrow descent and the Singer rocked and rolled on its old fashioned suspension, the tyres squealing as Roy fought with the steering, but the car stuck there and they gained on JP who, despite riding hard wasn't getting away and the circular drop of the ramp also meant that both pursuer and pursued could not go too quickly.

Butch gripped the elbow rest on the inside of the door, an expression of pure glee on his face. 'I'm enjoying this.'

He glanced at Roy who was totally focused on driving, but shouted, 'Me too.' He was beaming.

They spiralled down four flights to the ground floor.

JP constantly checked over his shoulder, riding as fast as he could, knowing that once he hit ground level, his escape was guaranteed.

He had one last look at the headlights of Roy's car, managed to jack up a middle finger, then looked ahead, his vision blurred and sparkly because of looking into the main beam, and because of this temporary issue he was too slow to react to the old Transit van that came from nowhere at 90 degrees to the ramp exit, blocking his path – with its sliding side door open wide like a hungry mouth.

JP could not brake in time. His BMX crunched head on into the lower edge of the van door, stopping its forward momentum instantly – but not JP's. He was hurled head over heels into the van, his arms and legs flailing. He smacked into the opposite side of the van with a thud and slithered semi-conscious down it like a jelly thrown at a wall.

Arthur was at the wheel of the van.

Richie slid out of the passenger side and slammed the sliding door shut, then climbed back in alongside Arthur as the van moved forwards, its rear wheel mounting and crushing the front wheel and forks of the BMX.

'There goes our no claims bonus,' Richie quipped.

Behind them, Roy's car ran over the rear wheel of the BMX and followed the van.

***

They were back at the unit, the van drawn up inside, Roy's car behind it.

Arthur was dragging a now gagged and bound JP towards a hoist, complaining, 'Jeez, my bloody back. I'm too old for this work.'

Butch asked if anyone wanted a brew.

The other three nodded, so he flicked on the kettle which was on a small table by the wall. He dropped tea bags into four mugs because, sometimes, only tea would do – especially if you were seventy years old.

157

Arthur dropped JP on the floor, then hooked the hoist to the bindings between JP's ankles and began to winch him, upside down, into the air until he swung like a black marlin on display on a quayside.

JP was now very much conscious and as soon as Richie ripped the gag off his mouth he shouted, 'What the fuck are you doin'? You're fucking dead, you got me, DEAD.'

He struggled against his restraints but all his effort served to do was make him sway like a broken pendulum, the top of his skull just skimming the floor.

'I'm alive and well,' Richie pointed out.

Roy stepped forwards, stopped JP from swaying then bent down next to him. Both of Roy's knee joints cracked hollowly and the other three exchanged glances of mirth. Roy held out a mobile phone and played the clip of Charlie being murdered.

'Remember this?'

JP didn't even bother to look at it, but continued to struggle and scream, 'Let me go, you bastards.'

'Look at it,' Roy insisted.

JP gave it a cursory glance. 'It ain't me.'

'Where can I find Aaron?' Richie asked quietly.

'Never heard of him.'

Richie and Roy took a step back and looked at Arthur who was now spinning a baseball bat in his hands, swishing it through the air with practise strokes, hitting an imaginary ball. He stepped in and struck JP on the back, over his kidneys, a blow that sent a shockwave of terrible agony through JP's body and made him scream.

'Now I'll ask you again ... or how do you lot say it? Aks you again? Where can I find Aaron?'

'Fuck you,' JP wheezed through clenched teeth.

It was Roy's turn. He winched JP's body up higher so that the young man's head was at about waist height, then he took out his Walther PPK and did something he hadn't had cause to do for many years. He pistol-whipped JP around the head, causing deep gouges and cuts in his skull and forehead and face, blood splattering the floor below with audible 'plops' as it landed.

'You see how this is going?' Richie said.

'You aksing me to rat out someone?' JP cried.

'I'm asking you how I find the person responsible for…'

'Fuck you. Whatever you think you can do, Granddad, you ain't as powerful as E2 … I grass on Aaron, I might as well be dead.'

Richie stared at him with lifeless eyes. Something about him changed as his hands bunched into fists and his whole body tensed up. He was on the verge of launching himself into JP, but the moment snapped when Butch came into his line of sight bearing a tray with four mugs of tea on it.

'Sounds very much like we're going to have to work through our tea break on this one,' Butch said, then, mock-confidentially to JP he said, 'The boss is a real task-master. He just wants to get the job done.'

'This is a joke,' JP said, pulling at his bindings, squirming. 'I know you ain't gonna do anything.'

'That's what your mates said last night,' Roy said.

JP stopped writhing.

'And guess what they're saying tonight, son?' Arthur asked. 'Nothing!' He roared with laughter at his own joke.

Richie began circling JP as he spoke, forcing JP to contort and turn to keep him in view. 'See, that's the trouble with your generation, JP. You think you are invincible. You think no one can touch you. You think if you do get caught, it's only a slap on the wrist. You think you're gonna live forever.'

Butch was already drinking his tea. He slurped it noisily and shrugged when they all gave him a dirty look. He said, 'But you won't live forever, pal.'

JP jerked around, looking at the four men who now surrounded him. 'Yeah,' he said boldly, 'well you better kill me now, cos when I get out…' He left the threat hanging.

'Jesus, look at you,' Butch chortled in his tea. 'This isn't some kind of Houdini trick.' He bent his knees slightly, bringing his eye line down to JP's. 'You're not getting out of this one.'

'When I…' JP started to say.

'When?' Arthur roared. 'You got to admire his optimism.

'When I get out, I'm gonna kill you all,' JP said and spat out a mouthful of accumulated blood from the deep cut inside his mouth.

'Now that's really funny, and a bit déjà vu,' Roy said. 'Spooky, cos that's exactly what Maz and Leroy said.'

'Right before we killed 'em,' Arthur screamed.

'When E2 find out about you,' JP persisted, 'you are fucked, and your bitches, wives, girlfriends, whatever ... they all gonna get fucked ... up the arse, up every fucking hole ... any of you got daughters or granddaughters?' he threatened. He caught Richie's eye. JP smiled through his bloodied face. 'You got a daughter? She won't be able to walk by the time E2 finished with her and you know what? She'll fucking love it.'

JP smiled, the blood coating his teeth.

Richie smiled back, but he was juddering with rage now, his heart racing madly.

'You know what irony is?' he asked JP, who looked blank. From his jacket Richie pulled out Charlie's knuckleduster and slid it over the fingers of his right hand, curling them comfortably through it so it nestled in his hand.

His fist shot out and smashed into JP's face. The brass connected with a loud, horrible crunch.

'This was my brother's,' he said.

JP spat out more blood, grinned and said, 'Well why don't you get on your knees, like he did, and start begging for mercy, like he did.'

Richie said nothing else. He just pounded his fist into JP's face again, feeling the cheekbone snap.

JP shook his head. He was feeling disconnected now, his brain having been jarred, pain radiating out from his face. But he continued, 'And we was laughing at him, laughing at your shit brother as we destroyed him.'

These were the last words he ever spoke.

Richie's wrath and his loss boiled up into an intense, unstoppable force and he exploded into JP with a flurry of blows, beating him around the head, jarring his own hand as he connected with the solid bone of the skull, or the softer flesh of the face, or the gristle of the nose, pummelling, pounding until he was himself breathless, his chest tightening as though there was a steel band wrapped around it.

Then, fury spent, he staggered away, finished.

JP hung there swaying slightly, but dead.

Roy lowered the body as Richie stood over it, panting. 'Jesus, this used to be easier.'

'So now what?' Arthur asked him.

'Now comes the main event … give me…' Richie started to say, but stopped as a pain unlike he had ever experienced before swept across his chest and zinged down his left arm to his fingertips.

He swayed, clutched his chest, his face suddenly a sickly grey colour.

'You okay, Richie?' Roy asked.

Richie grabbed his own left arm, groaned and staggered. The other three caught him before he hit the floor.

SIXTEEN

Time suddenly meant nothing to Richie Archer. He was caught up in a treacly whirlpool of flashing street lights, worried but incoherent voices, a horn sounding impatiently, a drumming in his ears … the shooting, all-encompassing pain from his chest and then the sensation of lying on his back seeing fluorescent light tubes zip by, crashing through double doors, worried faces, and the thought that maybe this was the route to hell – and who the fuck was he going to meet? Then there was nothing but blackness for a very long time; blackness that could have been death, then some kind of floating peace, then pain again, then it receding … pinpricks in his arms and the back of his hands. His eyes flickering open, three people looking down at him he didn't recognise and him saying one word, a name through a dry throat … 'Carmen.'

Then he surfaced, knew he was alive and the corridor he had been pushed along wasn't the road to hell, but to the intensive care unit.

'What happened?' he asked thickly.

'Heart attack,' a nurse said.

'Serious?'

'Are they ever just a joke?'

***

Once stabilised he was transferred up to the relative peace of the coronary care unit known as the 'Rankin Ward' on the third floor of the hospital and placed in a room with four beds, only his occupied, hooked up to various machines monitoring his functions.

A nurse smiled warmly at him.

'So I'm still here?'

'Very much so,' she said.

She glanced towards the door where three very worried faces were crushed up to the circular window. She beckoned them in. Roy, Arthur and Butch shuffled mutedly into the room.

'I'll be back in a moment,' the nurse told them. 'No excitement, okay?'

Arthur leered at her in a slightly scary way. 'How can there be no excitement with you walking around?'

She sighed. 'And they say chivalry is dead.' She left, aware that Arthur's eyes were with her all the way, so she gave her hips a little added sway.

The three friends surrounded the bed, one each side.

'How are you feeling?' Butch asked Richie.

Arthur was inspecting the monitors, his fingers hovering over buttons, fingernails tapping screens.

'Like a truck just ran over me,' Richie said, 'but also vulnerable here … I'll be glad when they get me on a proper, public ward.'

'I was thinking the same thing. This place is out on a limb and wide open,' Roy agreed.

'You're worryin' for nothing. Even if they knew you was here, they haven't got the balls to show,' Arthur said. He wrapped his hand around a tube from a drip, wondering what would happen if he squeezed it. It was just a passing thought.

'Maybe, but I don't fancy having to sleep with one eye open.'

'Then leave it to us, we'll sort it, matey.' Butch offered.

Richie shook his head which was back to thinking straight. 'No, I've got unfinished business with this little scrote, Aaron. If anybody's gonna do 'im, it's gonna be me.'

'So what's the plan?' Roy asked.

'Find me a phone. I need to call a friend.'

Butch handed over his mobile phone.

***

It was a Russian made Makarov 9mm semi-automatic pistol with a 10 round detachable box magazine, the standard Soviet military and police sidearm between 1951 and 1991. Although this particular one had seen much better days – it had even been fired in the Russian invasion of Afghanistan in 1979 – it was still reliable and would kill efficiently and without remorse.

At that moment it was pointed directly at Dean's head.

He swallowed and his mouth sagged open and he could very easily have shit himself, particularly as the person pointing it at him, whose finger was wrapped around the trigger, was Aaron.

Dean saw the cruel smile playing on Aaron's twitching lips.

And then he fired.

Click.

Dean flinched. He knew – or at least he thought he knew – the gun wasn't loaded, but even having an empty firearm pointed directly at his head had been, almost, a bowel emptying moment, especially with the psychopathic Aaron holding the thing.

Dean breathed out.

'Fuckin' wuss,' Aaron said contemptuously, then turned back to the table on which was arranged an array of firearms of varying makes, models and condition.

The gaggle of other E2 members clustered into Aaron's tower block flat sniggered at Dean, who shot them a warning look to shut it.

There was another man in the room. He was known only as 'The Russian', although to be honest no one was completely certain as to his true origin. He was tall and rangy, probably in his mid-forties, and he had the chisel-like Slavic looks of an East European and some said he used to be in the Russian military intelligence, the GRU, but that was only a rumour, one that the man himself did not try to deny. What was fact, though, was that he operated on the fringes of the London underworld, kept himself to himself, and provided a service. He was a gun dealer and based on Aaron's fairly meagre budget, he had brought along appropriate weapons to trade for cash.

'They all work?' Aaron wafted a hand at the display.

'Yez ... all servized by me. Zey work,' he said in a thick Russian accent that, in reality, he had lost a long time ago but continued to use for effect. He didn't blink.

Aaron looked at The Makarov, rotating it appreciatively in front of his face appreciatively. He smiled, picked up a fully loaded magazine and slammed it into the gun. 'Man, I shoulda got one o' these ages ago ... no one gonna mess wiv E2 now.' He pushed a pile of bank notes across the table towards The Russian, payment for the weapons, and said, 'My life savings bro ... but it's worth it.' He tossed a revolver over to Dean and said, 'Yours, man.'

The Russian counted the cash carefully, betraying no emotion despite the fact that because the weapons he provided had been to many hells and back, his mark-up was about 600%. He had bought them very cheaply indeed. He nodded.

There was a knock on the flat door – coded: rat-at-rat-at-at.

Aaron and the E2 froze for a moment. One of the gang peered through the spy hole, then opened up.

The Russian exited without a further word and DK and Lauren entered the flat.

Aaron's expression betrayed the fact he could not believe that Lauren was here. He looked questioningly at DK.

Dean looked dismayed.

'She doin' here?' Aaron said.

'She wanted to see you ... came to me,' DK said.

'An' you brought her here? She ain't never been here before.'

'I know ... but listen to her, man,' DK said.

'What the fuck d'you want, piggy?'

Lauren was actually terrified, but she fought to retain control of herself, though the sight of all the guns filled her with dread, another step up in an already dangerous situation and whereas Dean had nearly filled his trousers moments earlier, Lauren was desperate to pee. Nor did it help when she saw Dean was here and, even worse, had one of the guns in his hand.

She controlled herself. She could do this. She had to do this for her own sanity and self-respect.

'I've got some information ... that old bloke, the one who's hunting you down?' She glanced at DK.

'What about 'im?' Aaron said.

'He's in hospital ... I heard my mum talking about it earlier, she didn't know I was there. He's had a heart attack or something.'

'Bullshit.'

'It's the truth, I swear,' Lauren insisted. This was the easy bit because it was essentially the truth, with the exception of having heard it from her mother.

'So what're you telling me for?' Aaron asked.

'Cos I thought you'd want to get him and cos...'

'Cos what, bitch? What did you think?'

Now came the harder bit – the real lies. Lauren slid up to Aaron like a purring cat. 'I thought you would like me again and y'know, we could...' she said coyly and ran a hand over his chest.

Aaron jerked away from her with disgust. 'Get your pig hands off me.'

Lauren drew back trying to look gutted and hung her head, knowing that Dean was glowering at her with hatred. It was imperative to avoid eye contact with him.

Aaron paced the room, trying to get his head around this new development, coupled with the fact that JP was now on his 'missing' register along with Maz and Leroy. It was all very worrying and what if the old man had somehow got to them ... if he had, which he could hardly believe, then he realised that he himself was next on the list and maybe the best thing would be to take the old cunt out and have done.

He stopped and said to Lauren, 'Ring the hospital, find out where he is.'

'But I...'

'Just do it,' he said, coming in close to her. It was time for the E2 postcode gang to move to another level.

Lauren took out her phone but the number of the hospital wasn't on her contacts list, so with dithering fingers and under the scrutiny of the E2 gathered all around her, she had to connect to Wi-Fi, then the internet and search for the hospital number.

Eventually she found it and dialled. As she waited to connect, her eyes flicked from one E2 to the next, but avoided Dean's eyes, who she knew were burning into her like a laser beam. She could feel his intense hatred and it was hurting her. She wanted to crumble and run, admit everything, but as soon as she had entered Aaron's lair, that was no longer an option.

'Hello ... hi, I'm trying to find out about a patient called Richie Archer ... yes, he's my uncle ... yes, heart attack ... he's on the Rankin Ward? Which one is that? Oh, the cardiac unit ... thank you so much,' she said sweetly, ending the call, then raising her face to Aaron. 'See, I told you.'

Aaron nodded, reassured, then addressed the E2. 'Get some troops together ... maybe it time we pay this old fuck a visit.' He snatched up the Makarov and grabbed Lauren by the arm. 'You coming with us, cunt.'

***

Aaron led a large group of E2 gang members up the curving pathway towards the entrance of the A&E unit which, because the hospital itself was due to be closed, operated on restricted hours. Had Richie had his heart attack an hour later he would probably have ended up on the other side of London. But, fortunately for him, he had made it to this hospital which – maybe in one of its final boasts before closure – had a good quality coronary care unit.

So the E2 advance on the hospital was not even caught on any CCTV cameras because they had been turned off and the only security in the hospital were two overweight security guards who spent most of their time in a nice, warm office, making occasional forays onto the corridors. Their jobs would go when the hospital closed.

Aaron was dragging Lauren with him. She was reluctant and he was getting very annoyed with her.

Her mobile phone rang. She disengaged herself from Aaron's grip and tried to answer the call. He turned on her angrily.

'The fuck you doing?'

'It's my mum,' she lied. 'If I don't answer … let me text her at least.'

'No chance.' Aaron grabbed her arm again, tighter this time, and yanked her along. 'You stay close, got me? And put this on.'

Aaron pulled out a black, tight-fitting lycra mask with eye slits and handed it to her.

'What?'

'Just put it on.'

She stared at it in disbelief, then put it over her head, adjusting the eye slits so she could see, and as she glanced around she saw that every other gang member was now wearing one, including Aaron and Dean.

Lauren quailed at the sight.

The gang looked terrifying with masks that clung tightly to the contours of their faces yet revealed no features. They were, literally, masks from hell. And somehow, she knew, she had to send that text through – and it wasn't to her mum.

***

The coronary care side room situated within the Rankin Ward was in semi-darkness. The nurse came in and made a check, was satisfied all was okay, then, job done, she smiled and with one last glance around, she left.

***

It wasn't remotely difficult to get into the hospital. The main entrance had a large, circular reception desk and although the hospital itself was still open, evening visiting hours were over and the whole place was now just staffed with a few admin staff and the medical staff, mainly nurses, who were concentrated on the wards. To get attention at the reception, a visitor was required to ring a bell as there was no one staffing the desk itself.

That, combined with lazy security, meant that E2 could have brought twice as many with them, and danced their way through reception and into the bowels of the hospital unmolested and unchallenged.

Behind the reception desk was the central lift, and either side of that, staircases.

Aaron scanned the notice board with a list of wards and their locations, plus a map of the building and said, 'Third floor.' Then using military style signals he sent half the E2, including DK, up the stairs whilst the remaining ones all crammed into the big lift.

As the doors closed, Aaron said, 'Weapons check.'

He pulled his Makarov out of his waistband and checked it, slipping out the magazine, reloading and cocking it. Dean also checked the gun he had ended up with, a very battered, nondescript six-shot revolver with the make and serial number burned off with acid. It had seen better days.

Aaron shoved Lauren back into the corner of the lift as it began to rise. He pulled his mask up above his mouth, then did the same with hers, and forced his lips down onto hers, kissing her harshly, their teeth clashing as he made a horrible grunting noise of passion. Lauren responded with equal passion, rubbing herself suggestively up and down his thigh which he had lodged between her legs.

Then Aaron pushed himself away from her, laughing, revelling in the power he wielded over her. Stupid bitch. He decided that later that night, she would get raped firstly by him, then by DK who had professed an interest in going down on Lauren. After that the remainder of E2 would have their fill like never before and if she was alive at the end of it, Aaron would strangle her to death ... the ultimate display of power. Choke, release ... choke, release ... choke.

He pulled his mask down over his face again.

Dean watched his leader, sickened by the display. Not long ago he had admired him. Now he despised him. And Lauren, too. What the fuck was she playing at? Double-crossing bitch! He felt sick to his guts.

Dean held his gun tighter. His rage made him want to scream, but he held back. 'Get this shit over with, then go,' he told himself.

When the lift doors cranked open on the third floor, Aaron glanced out along the corridor and saw the entrance to the Rankin Ward.

He stopped.

This was the moment when the enormity of what was going on, what he was responsible for and what might happen in the next few minutes zapped Aaron like a ray gun.

He had a gun. His gang had guns – and now this had gone beyond a group of youths battering innocent people, or dealing drugs; he had led them into a hospital, sneaked through corridors and he was intending to murder someone in cold blood by blowing his head off. This was no accidental encounter. This was a pre-planned mission. What was the word, he thought fleetingly. Premeditated – that was it. And if it went wrong and he was caught for this, there would be no sweeping it under the carpet, no second chances. This time he would go to prison for a long, long time. A very unsettling sensation whizzed through his legs and he realised he was metaphorically shitting himself at the thought of being in a bigger man's game.

He was dithering, starting to bottle out, but he tried to fudge his way through this by making what he hoped looked like a decision a proper leader would make.

Delegation.

DK and another E2 member rounded the corner from the stairwell, breathing heavily from the exertion of running up three flights.

'Okay?' Aaron said.

'Yeah – no one on the stairs,' DK reported efficiently.

Aaron took DK by the shoulder and looked into her eyes behind the slits of her mask. 'DK? You wanna step up? Now's your chance.'

He tried to hold his voice steady, but there was a tremor in it.

'You want me to do it?' she responded with surprise.

He shook her. 'You fuckin' heard me. You wanna be a leader or a fuckin' sheep? You got potential, girl.' He looked at the E2 behind her. 'Both of ya – go!'

DK and the E2 glanced uncertainly at each other, then she made the decision, grabbed the lad, spun him round and went towards the ward doors.

Aaron watched, then caught Lauren's look, and even though she was wearing a mask he could tell she could not believe what he'd just done – sent someone else in to do his dirty work. He did not even remotely convince her when he said, 'You don't have a dog and bark yourself.'

The accusation that the murdered Charlie Archer had made to Aaron before he had been kicked to death suddenly resonated with Lauren. The old man had called him a coward – and he had been correct.

Aaron was a coward and the reality of that hit Lauren hard … but she had no time to dwell on it.

Things were moving quickly.

More E2 members appeared up the stairs, assembling and unsure what was next.

'You find another way in and out,' Aaron told three of them, making a circling gesture with his finger. 'Round the back.' To the others he said, 'You lot, hold this area – see no one comes up the stairs.'

Three broke away to search and see if there was another way into the ward.

Lauren took the opportunity to glance in Dean's direction and to shake her head and make him understand, but he turned away, rejecting her.

***

DK and the other E2 opened the swinging, double entrance doors to the Rankin Ward silently, then contorted through the gap and found themselves on a short corridor. On their left was a nurses' office, the murmur of someone talking, maybe on the phone.

On the name board by the door the name 'Archer, R' was written in felt tip pen next to 'Room 2.'

DK and the E2 ducked and sneaked low past the nurse's office door, and Room 2 was just ahead of them.

DK paused outside the door, her back pressed against the wall, trying to control her breathing. She slid slowly down to her haunches and took the pistol that had been given to her from her waistband. She had also been given a stubby silencer, which she slotted onto the muzzle with a firm click.

She, too, knew, this was the biggest moment of her short life, and the most dangerous, yet she also knew this was what could either make or destroy her and she was determined that it would be the former … she would be the one who had done the business when called upon.

She glanced back at the E2 by her shoulder, then pulled off her mask, indicating the lad should do the same.

'He needs to see our faces when he dies,' she whispered.

She rose back up to her full height, extended her left arm across the door and started to ease it open, then she slithered into the room which was still half-lit and peaceful.

There were sleeping patients in all four beds in the room, with name boards over each, but the one with the name Archer was in the far corner.

DK and the E2 crept towards it and stood at the foot of it, seeing the outline of the body under the covers, the connections to the monitors running out from under the sheets to the readouts and displays showing a good, steady heart rate and blood pressure.

DK swallowed and raised the pistol, aimed it at the body mass. She supported the gun with her left hand, though there was a slight tremor: her first kill and the one thing that would make her a postcode gang legend.

She pumped six bullets into the sheets, the entry of each slug making the body underneath jerk obscenely.

At six, the magazine emptied … she had known she only had six to start with … and the gun clicked: empty.

DK then had only the tiniest moment to revel in her victory – because suddenly all the lights in the room came on brightly.

DK shaded her eyes and spun as Richie Archer stepped out from what had been deep shadow by the door. He was dressed in black from head to foot and at hip level he held the sawn-off shotgun aimed squarely at DK, who froze.

Despite himself, Richie could not resist saying, 'You could've just brought flowers.'

Then, like a nightmare, the other three beds all came to life as the sheets were thrown back and three fully dressed men, all in black suits with black ties and black shiny shoes, sat up.

Butch was armed with his Kukri.

Roy had a revolver in each hand.

Arthur, in an effort to out-do the others, brandished an old fashioned Sten gun which needed strong hands and a lot of experience to handle.

All the weapons were aimed at DK and the E2.

DK dropped her gun with a crash, the E2 hovered to one side of her.

'You seen one of these before?' Arthur asked proudly of the Sten gun. DK and the E2 shook their heads and all four men feigned disappointment. 'Well let me tell you, it'll fuckin' hurt when I pull the trigger.'

'There more of you outside?' Roy asked.

DK nodded, now terrified and incredulous at how wrong it had all gone. How fucking hard should it be to kill an old codger?

'How many are there?' Richie asked. When neither responded, he shouted, 'Answer the fucking question!' Then, sideways to Arthur, he said, 'Put some eyes on the back, just in case…'

Before he could finish talking, the E2 pushed DK out of the way, his hand went to his back jeans pocket and he fumbled for the small revolver in there. This was going to be his moment.

Richie killed him with both barrels before the gun was even half way out.

SEVENTEEN

'That was a fuckin' shotgun,' Aaron gulped at the unmistakeable sound he'd just heard from within the ward. Panic coursed through him, but then a realisation hit him just as hard as the shotgun blast when he turned and looked into Lauren's face. She had just lifted her mask up and everything about her expression yelled guilt.

He spun on her, pinned her against the wall and held her there with one arm, whilst he took her phone from her and scrolled quickly through the texts, seeing one that instantly proved his suspicion.

It read, 'ITS ON NOW!'

It had been sent to someone called Butch.

'You bitch, you got us set up,' he said and with the power of a coward he smacked her hard, open-handed across the face, whipping her head around with the force of the blow and knocking her to the floor.

In that moment, Dean also realised exactly what was happening and hurled himself against Aaron and pushed him away from Lauren.

Aaron staggered away but kept his balance and found himself taken by surprise for the second time in less than a minute – firstly by the double-dealing of Lauren and then, worse, by the betrayal of one of his most trusted friends.

'What's this? Ya fucked up, Dean.'

Aaron raised the Makarov, almost point blank at Dean's unprotected chest, about to shoot Dean's heart to pieces, but before he could quite steady himself to fire, the double doors of the Rankin Ward burst open and a wheelchair shot out into the corridor with the figure of a body on it, covered by a bed sheet.

Aaron wheeled around, not understanding what he was looking at, just seeing it (rightly, as it happened) as an enemy tactic. Without thinking he opened fire at the figure, and the rest of the E2 who were arced in a semi-circle alongside him, opened fire too.

The firing stopped on Aaron's signal. Smoke rose from all the muzzles.

The sheet over the figure was torn and perforated with bullet holes and, now, seeping blood.

Aaron whipped the blanket away and threw it to one side and discovered to his mounting hysteria that underneath was the bound and gagged DK who had now been shot to death by her own gang, her muscled body a bloody, terrible mess of gore.

'Shit,' Aaron exclaimed.

Then, as all this was sinking in, one side of the double door to the ward opened and Roy stepped out, armed with his two pistols, firing in what appeared to be a crazy, haphazard way, but he was in fact shooting above the heads of the cluster of the E2 gang. They scattered like cockroaches in the light, most diving for cover back down the stairwell, including Aaron. They fell in a comical tangle of legs and arms and heads.

As quickly as he had appeared, Roy withdrew and the doors of the ward clattered shut.

Dean hauled Lauren for cover into the lift. The blood soaked blanket that Aaron had pulled off DK and thrown to one side had landed across the threshold of the lift doors and was preventing the doors from shutting. Dean had been forced to fling Lauren pretty roughly down as the bullets zipped and whizzed above his head, but he had then leapt on top of her, spreading his body to protect her from any ricochets. She was face down, trapped with his weight on her back, his head and hers together, their cheeks touching when Dean pulled off his lycra mask.

Through the side of her mouth she managed to say, 'I'm sorry if you thought...'

'Don't worry, I get it.'

'I do really like you,' Lauren felt it necessary to confirm.

'And I like you ... and as second dates go, this is pretty memorable.'

175

Although stuck under him, and in a very dangerous situation, she smiled … and then she saw her mobile phone which Aaron had dropped between the lift doors when the bullets had started flying. She wriggled towards it and grabbed it as Dean eased himself off her.

***

Arthur had been tasked to check out the hospital corridor that ran at the back of the Rankin Ward. He slid along with his back to the wall, the Sten gun cocked and ready in his hands.

There was a noise, unidentifiable.

He stopped, held his breath, listened, head cocked. He could feel sweat drenching him under his armpits, flowing down his bald head into his eyes and down the back of his head onto his neck and down between his shoulder blades. He had always been known as the heaviest sweater in Richie's gang and when the salty water flowed he knew he was in business and in his element – danger. He hadn't felt so good and alive in over twenty years. He just hoped his ticker wouldn't do a 'Richie' and give him problems. That said, he trusted the statins and blood pressure pills he now took each day. And he felt very much alive, the Sten gun feeling like some sort of lithe monster waiting to be unleashed.

Another noise … it could have been a whisper or a footfall.

A crouching, black-masked figure appeared at the next turn in the corridor, gun in hand, and 'bang', a slug thudded into the wall just by Arthur's ear. He ducked instinctively, dropped into a combat crouch, swung the Sten gun around and jerked the trigger back, loosed off half the magazine. The heavy calibre slugs gouged a perfect arch in the wall near to the turn causing the gun-toting E2 to scream in terror and dive for cover.

'Fuckin' sneaky fuckers,' Arthur said through gritted teeth, looking through the rising gun smoke from the end of the red hot barrel, his eyes blazing as he inhaled the aroma of a fired weapon which brought back so many blood-filled memories.

He smiled crookedly.

***

All of Richie's muscles contracted hard when he heard the blast of Arthur's gunshots. He recognised the sound of the Sten gun and hoped to hell that Arthur hadn't come off worse, although he doubted that.

The sound of gunfire died down.

Richie had reloaded his shotgun. He stepped over the shredded body of the E2 who'd had the temerity to try and shoot him, and said to Butch, 'Is there another entrance to this place?'

Butch was holding the Kukri at his side. 'Dunno, I'll go and have a look.'

'Don't do anything stupid,' Richie told him.

'As if.' Butch twisted out of the room and onto the ward, turning away from the main entrance and hurrying down past the patients in the open section of the ward, all now awake and afraid, the night nurse trying to calm them down.

All talk stopped abruptly as Butch ran past and all eyes watched in complete disbelief at the sight of the one man and his knife jogging past.

He ran past the toilets and shower rooms and came to an emergency exit door which he opened quietly, steeping into a dark corridor beyond. He stopped, now breathing heavily, listening. He began to make his way silently along this corridor, pressed tight to the wall, the Kukri ready to strike.

At a 90 degree turn in the corridor he stopped, instinct taking over, his mind fully concentrated. He knew he was dealing with amateurs, but they had proved themselves to be deadly, without conscience and willing to engage in violence. It was a long time since Butch had faced such people and he wasn't going to underestimate them.

He stood rock still.

Time ticked on.

He ran his tongue around his lips, tasting the salt of his sweat on his upper lip, and the dryness at the back of his throat.

He did not move.

Then his patience was rewarded as a hand holding a pistol snaked out from the corner … yes, he thought. He knew they had been there and they might have sensed he was there too … but he was the professional and could have waited all night long for them to show. As it happened, he'd only had to wait a minute.

Ahh, he thought … the impetuous nature of youth.

The hand with the gun extended, half the forearm now revealed.

Now it was the moment for Butch to move. He raised the Kukri and slashed it down on the exposed arm, just above the wrist.

The Kukri did its job.

Slicing through bone, gristle and flesh as easily as cutting paper, the extraordinarily finely honed blade swept through the E2's arm in one easy movement.

The E2 reared back, screaming, clutching the stub of the arm which pumped blood and the hand, still tightly gripping the gun, dropped to the floor, the forefinger jerked back and pulled the trigger, firing one shot harmlessly into the wall opposite.

The injured E2 turned, spraying blood across his fellow gang members behind him who cowered away, horrified as the hot red liquid splattered them.

Butch retreated fast before they could get themselves reorganised and come for him. At most, he guessed, he would only be able to slice off three more hands before they overpowered him.

***

Arthur was back on the ward as Butch returned, having pushed an empty bed across the emergency exit doors which he had re-locked, but knew that when the gang got to the doors, it would only impede their advance momentarily.

Butch ran up to Richie, Roy and Arthur. 'There's more of them coming,' he panted, wiping the blade of the Kukri on a paper towel.

The four men gathered behind the main entrance to the ward.

'There's loads of them – and I mean shit-loads,' Arthur said as he reloaded the Sten, slapping in a new magazine.

Then, as bullets slammed into the doors from the opposite side, splintering wood, shattering glass, the four threw themselves to the floor.

'Jesus, this lot can't take a hint,' Butch whined.

***

Susan Taylor sat back at her kitchen table and took a sip of her white wine. Not too much. She was looking over the Archer murder file and wanted to keep her head reasonably clear. She picked up a sealed envelope addressed to her from the Technical Support Unit, opened it and sifted out the contents. The covering letter told her that what was enclosed were a series of still photos downloaded from the CCTV camera in the Chicken Hut. She was the first to see them.

She put the letter to one side and looked through the pictures, taken from the camera she had seen when she'd peered through the window of the premises, the camera affixed behind the counter.

They were just a bunch of photos taken throughout the evening of the murder, recording the clientele.

'Shit,' she said, as she looked at one showing a young couple canoodling at one of the tables. 'Oh my God ... what the..?' She reached for her wine, necked it and then, with a trembling hand reached for her mobile phone which started to vibrate just as she picked it up.

She saw the caller was Lauren.

Even before her daughter could say anything, Taylor snapped, 'You had better be on your way home...'

'Mum!' Lauren said desperately, calling from the hospital lift, 'I think I might need your help.'

***

They were taking cover down on the floor. Richie was half-propped against the wall, holding the shotgun. Roy was opposite, guns in hands. Arthur lay flat on his quite big stomach, the Sten gun trained on the doors. Butch was on his haunches, his eyes searching for some kind of advantage.

His eyes lit on a gas bottle on a trolley. He shuffled across to it opened the regulator so the gas started hissing out, then started pushing it towards the ward doors, building up speed and momentum as he went until he crashed it through the doors. As it burst through, he grabbed Riche's shotgun and fired both barrels into the bottle. The regulator flew off and clouds of compressed gas filled the corridor with an instant mist.

Butch ducked as Roy rose and fired into this mist-screen, but gunfire was returned and Roy teetered back into the ward, clutching his arm, hit and hurt.

***

In the corridor the gas bottle expended all its contents and Aaron, from being stressed and afraid, was in a frenzy of excitement.

He was the one, he believed, who had fired at and hit one of the old gangsters. Truth was, thorough the cloud of gas it could have been any one of the E2 who had winged him, but Aaron was the one taking the credit.

'I popped him,' he declared excitedly. 'I popped him.' He got to his feet and started to dance like a demented marionette as he celebrated his first hit. 'I popped him, I popped him.'

But behind him, another member of the gang was seeing the reality of the situation. 'We gotta get out, man,' he said to Aaron, trying to bring him back to earth. 'Feds be comin' … they gotta be.'

***

Roy sat propped up in the ward, holding his shoulder, his face screwed up in pain. Richie sat beside him, dour and worried now.

This was all down to him. His thirst for revenge that had dragged his four – old, very old – mates into a perilous situation from which there might be no good outcome. That they'd hitched a ride willingly was no compensation for Richie. Of course they'd follow him to hell. Of course they'd put their lives on the line because that's what they'd done for him – and he for them – all their lives since being teenagers. But Richie was starting to believe he should not have asked them in the first place. The world was different now and they were just four old guys who'd lived their glory days.

'You okay, Roy?' he asked. Whatever size of slug had hit him had taken a big old chunk of material from his sleeve and a very nasty wound was exposed. Blood ran down the inside of the clothing and covered Roy's right hand.

Roy had seen and read the expression of doubt on Richie's face.

'We wouldn't be here if we didn't want to be,' he told Richie quietly, and gave him a pointed look. Then he shouted, 'I will be okay if someone can reload this bleeder.' He held out a revolver with his good hand. Richie took it with a wry grin, broke it open and started to reload it with shells from Roy's jacket pocket.

Arthur was at the door. He pushed it open with his foot, stuck the muzzle of the Sten through the gap he'd created, and loosed off half a magazine into the corridor beyond, then dropped back quickly as a hail of fire came back at him, shredding the door, shattering glass. Crouched over, being hit by flying debris like hailstone, Arthur said, 'We need to stop 'em getting in here.'

He signalled for Butch to accompany him, then the two of them scrambled down the ward and turned into the room Richie had been occupying, where the dead E2 gang member still lay. Together they manoeuvred and wheeled out one of the empty beds and ran it up against the inside of the main ward doors.

The two men exchanged a glance of satisfaction, then Butch said, 'I need to go check the door at the far end … we're under siege, matey.'

As he ran through the ward, again past the clustered and terrified patients, he drew his own firearm out of his waistband.

In the short corridor beyond the door against which Butch had previously wedged a bed, two masked E2's had sneaked up and were tentatively checking the door, finding it wedged.

One of them rose slowly, taking a chance to peep through the square glass window in the door. This was something he should never have done as Roy was waiting on the other side and as he saw the masked face appear, there was no hesitation.

He shot him through the glass.

***

Lauren and Dean were still in the lift. She was frantically banging her finger against the buttons in the hope of closing the door, but Aaron stepped in and kicked Dean in the face, sending him sprawling.

Lauren stopped what she was doing and Aaron grabbed her by the hair and hauled her to her feet.

***

Inside the ward, Richie had helped Roy to peel off his jacket to expose the shoulder wound. The bullet had gouged through the muscle, leaving a deep cut but it looked as if it was 'only' a flesh wound. That said, a flesh wound in the arm of a man Roy's age could have a devastating effect and Richie looked worriedly at his old mate whose pallor had turned corpse-grey and who was bathed in sweat as he fought valiantly against the agony. Richie tore open the shirt, his eyes constantly moving to Roy's face and back to his task.

'Fuck,' Roy said. 'Cost me two hundred nicker, that shirt.'

Arthur crouched beside them, eyeing the wound. 'No excitement, my arse,' he laughed.

Butch came to join them. 'Old Bill are gonna be all over this like a rash soon.'

182

'Can't say I'll be sorry to see them, either,' Richie said dourly, dabbing carefully at Roy's wound with a piece of his shirt sleeve, making his friend wince.

'Stop firing, stop firing,' they heard a voice call from the other side of the door.

Aaron's voice.

'I got your inside traitor,' Aaron shouted. 'You hear me? I'm gonna blow her fuckin' head off unless you come out right now, you hear me?'

EIGHTEEN

Taylor was at the wheel of her car, throwing it through the streets of East London, cutting up other drivers, overtaking recklessly and slowing down only marginally to zoom through red lights. She was on speakerphone to DC Graham Watts who already happened to be en route to the hospital – he'd been in the office when the control room began getting calls from various sources reporting gun shots from the hospital and had turned out. A firearms team from the Metropolitan Police's CO19 department who had been about to go off duty had simply jumped back into their personnel carrier and shot off to the scene.

'Where we up to, where we up to?' Taylor demanded.

Watts pulled into the hospital grounds behind the firearms vehicle – they had already debussed and were entering the building, tooled up, firearms ready – and skidded to a halt.

'Armed units already on the scene, Guv ... currently securing the lower floor,' He had one ear to the radio channel dedicated to the firearms team.

'Do we have any information on what's happening?'

'Not yet ... still reports coming in of gunfire, but nothing more than that...'

'My daughter's in there,' she said anxiously.

'She's smart enough to keep her head down,' Watts reassured her.

'And dumb enough to get involved,' Taylor murmured to herself as she mounted the kerb with two wheels, scattered a group of kids, bounced back onto the road and ran another red light. The image of Lauren and Aaron sitting in the Chicken Hut stuck in her mind.

***

'I mean it,' Aaron screamed dementedly. He now held Lauren by the scruff of her neck, the muzzle of the Makarov screwed hard into the side of her head. 'You've got five seconds.' He began a countdown. 'Five … four…'

***

Richie was on his feet. Roy was propped up, his shoulder bleeding profusely. Arthur and Butch looked at Richie.

He simply shrugged, then shouted to Aaron. 'Okay, I'm coming out.'

'Are you fucking mental? It's suicide,' Butch said.

'Got no choice, she's just a kid,' Richie said, thinking, 'Someone else I've got involved in these shenanigans,' but he did not say it out loud.

'She might not even be there for all we know,' Arthur warned him.

'I can't take that chance. You know I can't.'

The four men looked at each other ominously.

'I mean it,' Aaron screamed. 'I'll kill the bitch.'

'Okay, we're coming,' Richie called back.

***

The firearms unit had secured the ground floor, put an armed cordon around the outside of the place with snipers taking up positions too, and were working their way systematically – and swiftly – up the hospital stairs from both end of the premises.

Watts was bringing up the rear – unarmed, of course, but with his bullet proof vest on.

***

Aaron waited, his gun still jammed into Lauren's temple.

Behind him, the E2 gang waited, some still covering the stairwell.

The ward door opened slowly and Richie led out Butch, Arthur and the wounded Roy.

Excitement gushed through Aaron at the sight of these four bedraggled old men limping out at his command – his command. He knew he had beaten them, these four silly old cunts who had dared to challenge him, and now he was going to take revenge – because wasn't this what it was all about?

But first things first.

'Get your hands where I can see them. No fucking tricks and slide your guns over here.'

One by one the men obliged. Richie allowed his shotgun to slide to the floor, then side-kicked it across the tiles to Aaron. Butch placed the Kurki down and slid it gently across. Arthur did the same with the Sten gun and Roy's two handguns.

Aaron grinned triumphantly, having torn off his mask. He pushed Lauren away to one side and pointed the Makarov directly at Richie's head.

'I told you old man, you's dead. But first you gotta watch me waste your boys.'

His gun arm, extended, pointed at each one in turn.

'You mean like we wasted your boys?' Richie said, knowing this was going to be like prodding an angry tiger with a shitty stick. A tiger that wasn't in a cage, at that.

Aaron's gun whipped back to point at Richie. He was furious for a moment, then he smiled.

'The E2 an army. The expendables. Lose one, another one come, takes his place.'

'Like cockroaches,' Richie said – another prod. 'Living in shit.'

'And what you got, Mister Old School Gangster? I tell you what you got … about thirty seconds … so, which one of these old guys you want me to shoot first?' He aimed the Makarov at Arthur who scowled back, unafraid. 'How about this bald old fat granddad?'

Before Aaron could say another word, Dean rushed out of the lift, shoulder charging Aaron to the floor with all the power he could muster. The Makarov spun from his grip and skittered to a point half way between him and Richie.

Richie moved fast, scooped up the pistol as members of the E2 dragged Dean and Lauren away from Aaron.

Richie clicked the magazine out.

Aaron scrambled to his feet, his knife appearing almost magically in his hand. He ran at Richie, screaming madly, who, despite the situation could not stop himself from releasing the magazine again and ramming it home for the second time.

Aaron was almost on him, the shiv catching a glimpse of light.

'Richie, just fucking shoot him,' Roy yelled, even though he was injured.

Aaron was on him now, the knife beginning its deadly arc.

Richie – furious with himself for not being able to overcome his 'thing' – threw the pistol down because he knew he had no choice about reloading it for a third time. At the last possible moment, he side-stepped and the knife slashed down within a hair's breadth of his cheek, and as Aaron stabbed fresh air, Richie pulled out Charlie's knuckleduster from his pocket, already fitted to his hand. He angled back as Aaron stumbled past, a victim of his own wrath and speed, slashing thin air. Richie turned almost like a ballet dancer, then transformed into a brutal street fighter and punched Aaron hard on the back of his head with the prohibited weapon. The knuckleduster immediately opened a deep gash in Aaron's skull and he cried out.

'That's from Charlie,' Richie informed him.

Aaron turned, tried to recover, swung a wild punch at Richie who again side-stepped, this time like a matador avoiding the horns of a charging bull, and he brought his fist around and smashed Aaron in the face, breaking his nose with a very satisfying crack.

Then Richie moved in and repositioned himself. He even had time to hold the now woozy and hurt Aaron steady for one more, major blow, the best one Richie had ever delivered in his life – hard, central, well-aimed, the business.

'And that's from me,' he said grimly.

He stepped forwards, powered another into Aaron's face, then another and he continued pounding until Aaron's face was a blood soaked, soggy mess.

The gang leader staggered backwards against a window, spitting and swallowing blood.

It was at that moment that Richie saw the red laser dot hovering over Aaron's chest – the dot used to aim a sniper rifle.

'Shit.' Richie dropped instantly to the floor, realising the danger from outside.

The firearms team poured up and out of the stairwell at that moment, weapons drawn, loaded and pointed, screaming instructions at everyone.

'Armed police, armed police. Hands in the air now!'

With one exception, every E2 gang member followed these words ... that exception being Aaron. He might have been punch drunk but he was still on a mission as his eyes set on one of Roy's discarded handguns which he picked up and started to wave about menacingly, not understanding the danger he was putting himself in.

Behind him, the window was shattered by the bullets from one of the police snipers positioned in the hospital grounds and Aaron's head was torn apart by .762 calibre slugs fired from an HK G36 rifle.

'And we have a winner,' Richie said as Aaron fell dead.

NINETEEN

Richie sat propped up in the hospital bed, now really attached to a monitor and drip. In the bed alongside him was Roy, having had his wound treated and bandaged expertly. Butch and Arthur sat on plastic chairs between the beds. They had been moved to a different room, as the one Richie had been in originally was now a crime scene with a dead body in it.

All four pairs of eyes were on DI Susan Taylor who was pacing angrily up and down the gap between the beds, and along the front of them.

Watts lounged by the door, arms folded, watching his boss with just a tiny grin playing on his face.

Taylor stopped suddenly, then held her head in her hands before lifting it up, stretching her tired features with her fingertips.

At that moment, when she dragged the lower section of her eyelids down, exposing the bloodshot eyes, Watts didn't think she was quite as pretty as she could be.

'Let me get this straight,' she challenged Richie. 'You seriously expect me to believe it was self-defence?'

'We told you what happened,' Richie said.

'We were all kippin' and these two come into the room, all tooled up, like,' Roy said. Now that he had been treated and a drip was running into his arm, he looked much better, not like he should be on a mortuary slab any more. He smiled at the DI: a lie with a lot of truth in it was always much harder to disprove than one that was a complete lie.

'And you took their guns off them? You?' Taylor said incredulously. 'Seventy year old men?'

'No need to be insulting, inspector,' Butch said.

Taylor looked daggers at each one in turn, unable to find the words, which was very unusual for her. She seemed to come to a decision, then turned to Watts. 'Give us a minute, will you?'

Watts left. He was glad, because he did not want to hear anything that might come back and bite him on the arse in the future.

When he'd gone, Taylor asked, 'Is this it?'

'I don't know what you mean,' Richie said.

'Listen, you … I've got every armed copper north of the Thames crawling around inside and outside this place, so if you want me to feed you to them, I will.' She paused, eyed him. 'Now, I'll ask you again – is this it?'

'I don't know what else to tell you, Inspector,' Richie said. 'All I know is that as soon as I'm discharged from here, I was planning to go back to Spain.'

Taylor nodded.

'Count your blessings, Inspector,' Richie said. 'You got clean streets again … I think the people around here deserve that, don't you?'

She sighed deeply, then headed for the door, where she paused and turned back. 'There is one final thing I have to say and if I don't say it now, I might not get another chance.'

'What's that?' Richie said.

'Thanks.'

'For what?'

'For saving my daughter, putting your life on the line to do so.' Her hand reached for the door handle.

'On that, kind of…' Richie said before she went.

She stopped, shaking her head. 'What?'

'My jacket hung up there?' Richie pointed to his suit jacket on a coat stand by the door. 'Left hand pocket … you'll find a piece of paper.'

Puzzled, Taylor slid in her hand and extracted a folded piece of paper, which she opened up. There was a name and address on it. She looked sharply at Richie who said, 'Did a bit of diggin' in my spare time,' he grinned ironically. 'You might want to check him out.' Taylor still looked baffled. 'Armed robbery quite a few years back at a newsagent … a good cop went down, I believe.'

Taylor's face changed dramatically with shock. 'Thank you,' she mouthed and left without another word before she burst into tears.

Richie raised his eyebrows. 'I have that effect on women,' he said.

***

Two days later, Richie scanned the clientele of the Dover Castle, grinning at the sea of happy faces. They were a group of folk who seemed suddenly to have had a huge weight lifted from their shoulders. They had got their manor back.

He was on the phone in the exact spot Charlie had occupied when the two brothers had last spoken and he was smiling as he chatted to the one person who had been the most important in his life for many years, loving the tinkling sound of her voice, imagining her beauty.

'So how is the East End now?' Carmen asked. She was sitting at a seafront bar in Spain.

'Quiet.'

'I could have come, you know … to the funeral.'

'You barely knew him … anyway, your life is out there.'

'And yours?' she asked, detecting something in his voice.

Richie did not reply. He looked around the pub as he thought about his possible answer, looked at his friends, then finally looked at Lizzy who happened to be wearing a red dress which made her look stunning.

'Are you getting homesick, or maybe you've met someone?' Carmen guessed.

Female intuition, Richie thought as he watched Lizzy fondly, a terrible thing. She was laughing infectiously, throwing back her head as Arthur said something to her, something completely inappropriate, Richie assumed. As her laugh faded, her eyes caught Richie's briefly, then returned to Arthur.

'I should be home for supper,' Richie said.

'Then I'll have something ready.'

'No. I'm bringing some pies for you to try … proper grub.'

'Ha, okay, looking forward to it … have a safe flight … love you, Dad.'

'Love you too.'

Richie hung up with a sigh. Roy, Arthur and Butch eyed him expectantly. He gave them the nod and they rose from around Lizzy and dispersed as Richie settled into one of the vacated seats.

There was a moment of hesitation, then Lizzy said, 'I won't come out. I hate goodbyes.' She wore a brave face but it was just a veneer to hide her sadness.

'We might have had a night in, but we never had that night out, did we?'

'Well, you got kinda busy.'

They both giggled like teenagers and it felt good. The laughter petered out and Richie's face turned serious. 'You can always come to Spain … I could do with a carer for a while.' He placed his hand over his heart – which, fortunately, was still pumping and the prognosis was good.

'Slave more like.' They laughed again and Lizzy went on, 'It's a lovely idea, but,' – she shrugged sadly – 'daughter, granddaughter … I couldn't leave 'em. This is home again, I belong here.'

'Well the offer is always there.'

They embraced tightly, reluctant to let go, and as they parted, Lizzy kissed him on the cheek.

'Take care, Richie.'

'My lady in red,' he whispered, stood up and headed for the door where he took one last look around. The locals all nodded a respectful thanks to him, but he didn't really see them. His focus was all on Lizzy.

***

'Good riddance to him,' Butch said crossly.

'Anyone that wants to ponce about playing golf in the sun rather than stay here isn't worth knowing,' Arthur said.

Butch, Arthur and Roy were standing side by side at the observation window adjacent to the airport terminal building.

The jet carrying Richie back to the sun had taxied to the end of the runway. They could hear the scream of the jets as the pilot built up power, then released the brakes and the plane thundered down the runway, rising into the evening sky.

Butch and Arthur looked at Roy, whose left arm was in a sling. He could physically feel their glares. 'I can tell you're not lying.'

They sniffed and looked out of the huge window again. The plane was already a speck in the sky and was banking towards the south.

'And I agree,' Roy said. 'After everything we've been through recently, he still turns his back on us.'

'Just like he did all those years ago,' Butch added.

'That's not fair!'

The three men spun to their right and saw that somehow Richie Archer had managed to sneak up on them, unseen and unheard, and stand alongside them facing out of the window. 'Way back then I was running from the Old Bill, keeping my head down, taking the heat off you mugs.'

'Who you calling a mug?' Butch reacted. He grabbed Richie and a mock fight ensued for a few moments, and the men laughed.

Roy was looking sardonically at him. Richie was Roy's oldest friend and he was confused. With narrowed eyes he asked, 'Why did you stay, then? Why didn't you actually get on that plane? Really? And don't try lying to me. I can see right through a lie.'

Richie gave a pained expression and by the time he was about to answer, the others had realised the truth and together they declared, 'Lizzy!'

Richie looked sheepish and dropped his eyes, a bit embarrassed. 'She might have something to do with it, yes.' He smiled conspiratorially. 'But there is something else.' He pursed his lips, then looked out across the runways through the picture window. Then he frowned, having seen a tiny smudge on the glass. With irritation he took out his handkerchief and rubbed away the mark. The others waited, knowing not to push him, and he continued, 'Tidying up our streets, getting rid of those low-life scum,' – he turned to Butch. 'You have got rid, haven't you?'

'You will never see those bodies again,' Butch assured him.

'Just checking … anyway … it's got my blood pumping. This is who I am, who we are.'

'Fuck me, where's this rambling speech coming from?' Arthur wanted to know.

'Too much time spent with poncy Europeans,' Butch said knowingly.

They all rocked with laughter, a good feeling between them, but suddenly, with just the merest switch of his body language, Richie turned serious. There was a coldness in his eyes and the others snapped their mouths shut, knowing when to keep schtum.

'Lizzy mentioned something to me, something about some of the pensioners in the manor having their life savings robbed off them.'

'Burglars?' Butch said.

Richie shook his head. 'Worse – bankers. I think we should teach them a lesson.'

They knew this was a serious proposition and each considered it.

'Do I get to kill any of them?' Butch ventured hopefully.

Richie smiled. He had always liked Butch's enthusiasm for drawing blood which obviously had not withered with age. 'Maybe, but I don't really think they'd care about that … I want to really hurt them,' he said wickedly.

'We're going to steal their money!' Arthur said, getting it.

'You remember that thing we did with Charlie back in 1969?' Richie said.

'Turin!' Roy exclaimed. 'How could we forget that? The gold heist.'

'Wait, wait, wait,' Butch cut in. 'You wanna steal their gold … how?'

Richie's eyes scanned all three, nodding reassuringly. 'Let me buy you all a drink … I've got a great idea.'

They turned as a line and walked out of the airport side-by-side, each man in a smart black suit, black shirt, black tie, black shoes, their smouldering presence ensuring they were given a wide berth by everyone, who watched open-mouthed, gawping as four grizzled, old grey wolves went on the hunt in a dog-eat-dog world.